Chapter 1

"What about Cordoba?"

Julia continued to reading the arts section. "Mmmm?" she mumbled.

"Cordoba...a long weekend for your birthday....it's in Spain."

Julia pushed herself up on her pillows and squinted over my shoulder at the travel guide. "I'd prefer Seville...more to see... and there'll be orange blossom everywhere in May."

"Yeah but Cordoba! It would be more intimate....*and*...they have the patio festival in May. Says here that May's the best time, you know, Espana in bloom and all that; *and* during this festival you can wander in and out of everyone's private patios and gardens; could be really interesting."

Julia sank back down and her face disappeared back into her bit of the paper. "How's the overdraft Callum?"

"Why do you have to *do* that?" I was already folding away our weekend with a sigh.

"Do what?" she mumbled "I was just asking."

I tossed it onto the bedroom floor. "Oh, well it's not too bad...I mean, it's not too good, but it's not desperate; well, not very desperate." That was that.

Julia and I had both taken what seemed at the time to be a pretty good offer of redundancy from the firm we both worked for. It seemed a good idea at the time, and gave us enough money to buy the flat with just a tiny mortgage; but we hadn't bargained on the employment situation, or to be more accurate the unemployment situation, and six months on we were hovering somewhere to the southern side of skint.

"I should've married Carol Worthington," I mused. "Loaded she is, and really had the hots for me; Cordoba….Seville…could've bought a little villa….one in each even."

"That's nice! You would've married *her* but you just shacked up with me! Mind you, you couldn't have married me anyway."

"Why's that?" I said, walking straight into it.

"Because…if you *had* asked…I'd have said no!"

"Oh," I said, crestfallen. Was I crestfallen, or was I putting it on, I wasn't sure. "Would you?" I turned to look at her, quizzical, accusatory, and surprisingly finding myself both sounding and feeling slightly hurt.

She snuggled in, adopting the little girl overly sweet voice: "Of course I wouldn't darling; and anyway, I thought the plan was that we *were* going to get married sometime."

Julia was at it. I knew she was at it but I just couldn't help trotting along. "Well yeah, of

course…*sometime*"

"But you have to ask then," she said, matter of fact and business like now; "I mean its standard practice….you have to ask…you never have."

"Don't be stupid," I said, "We've been living together for a million years!"

"Yes Callum but that's not the point, you can't just assume, even if we both agree. You're the man, and you have to ask," she declared. I sometimes thought that Julia would have made a very good schoolteacher. "Oh go on darling," she whinged, nuzzling her head into my neck, the voice still just that little bit too sweet, "Just for me, it would mean such a lot to me."

She was stroking my hair and edging her leg up between mine...right up between mine. I succumbed.

"OK, alright, are you ready," I said, and she sat up straight, eyes innocent wide and a little voice.

"Yes."

"I'm not going down on one knee," I said.

"No," (little voice), "that's alright."

I cleared my throat: "Will you marry me?"

"NO!" she proclaimed in a very silly high voice and jumped out of bed with a flourish, "I think I'll have a shower."

But I was out too and grabbed the shared bath robe before she could:

"Frankly my dear, I don't *give* a damn!" and I was off and away, but had the nagging doubt that it may have been nearer Vivien Leigh than Clark Gable.

Coffee and the business news; I liked Sunday mornings still, even though we could do this every day if we wanted to, and sometimes did. There was a niggling irritation today though, interfering with my concentration. 'Miners bounce back' in the Footsie report brought to mind momentarily an image of the seven dwarves bouncing along home where Snow White reclined in a negligee ready to receive them; lucky dwarves. We were having another Sunday morning without sex. I quickly counted up....that made three on the trot (bounce?), four even...well it was a few anyway. What was it? Was there a strand of negativity running through the usual banter, or was I just smarting slightly having been outmanoeuvred so comprehensively?

A flick on my ear: "Oi you! You haven't left me any coffee!"

"Oh, sorry darling," I said, "I'll make us a fresh pot".

"Don't worry darling" (loving kiss on forehead...she was rubbing it in), "I'll do it; you enjoy your Business... though I'll never understand why you read the business news when we're poor as church mice. Anyway, what's happening?"

She crossed to the sink and I saw that she had a towel turban and, as was her wont, had wrapped the bath towel around her at the waist like a man... only distinctly not. I never was quite sure if it was a deliberate tease or just a declaration of total familiarity and all that goes with it; despite experiencing a distinct twitch I returned to the paper.

"The miners are bouncing back".

"What do you want to do today?" I asked without raising my head as we settled into our second cup.

"Call*um*!" Julia had a habit of using my name as a rebuke which I sometimes worried might be having an adverse effect on my already fragile self-esteem. She chanted: "Henry's? Ray and Sian? Sian's birthday? *You* arranged it!"

Of course! I was immediately cheered up. Henry's was a jazz pub that did rather good Sunday afternoon sessions, and I had arranged to meet our friends Ray and Sian there for a few drinks to celebrate Sian's birthday.

Toast, yet more coffee, and further shuffling through the enormous Sunday paper which seemed to grow ever more parts; I wondered at this and the ever increasing litter of junk mail that dropped through our letter box, about all the trees they must have to chop down, and how they managed to grow enough of them so quickly to support these excesses.

Julia had evidently tired of the paper and I sensed that she was looking at me but didn't look up. "Let's go back to bed for a while," she said, quietly. I looked up. Julia was sitting back straight and bare breasted less than an arm's length away like a latter day Salome; I felt a sudden and unexpected thrill.

"OK," I said, nonchalantly, stretched and headed perhaps a little too eagerly for the bedroom as Julia rose too, but paused to rummage through the paper:

"I'll just find the crossword…"

Chapter 2

By the time we got to Henry's Ray and Sian were ensconced in one of those little velvety booths with a good view of the band that performed on a small dance floor, leaving just enough room for tipsy dancing later on. Kisses for the girls, and Julia sat down next to Sian, Ray accompanying me to the bar. Julia was holding forth straight off and the lovely Sian (known as such to the boys) was listening with that slightly dreamy air that always made you wonder if she really was.

The bar was busy.

"Alright?" Ray said. He was a man of few words but a whiz with computers with whom he communicated intimately and with a level of understanding that was virtually symbiotic. He'd moved swiftly and with apparent ease from the technical side to management, quite senior now and amply rewarded... so I had no hesitation in letting him buy the drinks.

"Yeah, not so bad" I said.

"You and Julia OK?" he said, dead pan. Was it just slightly blunt social skills, or did Ray really have some form of second sight?

"Yeah fine" I said, "Happy as paupers in a sinking ship."

He laughed and shouted our order over the heads of the line of blokes at the bar.

"So what about Sian then, how old is she?" I said with the customary directness of old mates who've played five a side and showered together for years.

"You must be bloody joking," he said in the cockney which always same through stronger when he was cursing. "She'd kill me if I told you."

"But she won't know," I said, "I'm not going to tell her."

"Thirty-eight," he said, reaching for the drinks.

"Christ!" I said, "really...thirty-eight...?"

"Bloody hell Callum, steady on, you and Julia are both past that aren't you, and I'm down right venerable by comparison!"

"Yeah I know", I said "But it just hits you when you see your friends getting older, and Sian...I've always thought of Sian as..."

"Yeah alright mate, I don't want to know about your dirty little fantasies." Ray knew that Sian was, to all the boys, "The lovely Sian".

When we got back to the girls Julia was still holding forth and Sian looked pleased to see us. I always had the feeling that Sian wasn't overly fond of Julia; not that she didn't like her as such, but just that they were on different plains so to speak. I think she preferred the company of the boys in general. Despite her fabled girly attributes, the lovely Sian was not a very girly girl. Girls and boys. Here we all were drifting rudderless into middle age, and we were still girls and boys.

I looked earnestly, almost sympathetically at Sian: "So my little chickadee..." my WC Fields was never anywhere near, but I never let that put me off... "You're thirteee" as I prolonged the last syllable I saw Ray's eyes widen as he pause mid sip of his lager "...what?"

He narrowed them now, apparently not seeing the funny side.

"Darling," Sian said with an intonation that suggested she was addressing a child for whom her fondness was habitually tested, "It's none of your bloody business."

"Oh."

"...and Callum,"

"Yes Sian?" I said with excessive solicitousness.

"If you're intending to wind me up all day about my age, I may just have to break your nose."

"Oh," I said again. "Well....Happy Birthday!" and Julia and I launched into a perfectly synchronised chipmunks rendition of Stevie Wonder's Happy Birthday to You. We'd done it before ad nauseum, and I was certain that Sian and Ray had both heard it on previous occasions, but they both still cracked an appreciative if sympathetic smile. Well, that's what friends are for?

All of this was par for the course. You know how people sometimes adopt specific personas with certain individuals, well with Sian I tended to clown about, and she in turn would respond in mock reproof. It was my defence mechanism because she was simply *so* gorgeous she made me slightly nervous; and today she had poured herself into a tight little number that had me instantly reaching for the quips.

Ray never danced. If there was a stock phrase used to describe Ray it would have been "Ray's alright." This sounds like faint praise, but in Ray's case it was invariably intoned with a sense of admiration....solid, dependable, capable, a good man for the crisis or the night out, not to say successful and moderately talented. Anchor man in our five a side team, he had an understated self-assurance alongside his quite dry, or as the Scots would say somewhat dour persona, which lent him an air of quiet authority. The girls liked him in a Humphrey Bogarde sort of way, but he had been with Sian since the ark, a catch even for old Ray. Shading fifty too, so 'old Ray' wasn't that far off the mark in the scheme of things with our crowd.

We went back a long way; pre Sian... early Julia. Yeah, he was alright, a good mate. He went his own way, supported Southend...collected Buddy Holly memorabilia (and quite an authority)...quirky stuff like that, but he did alright too... money, posh Mercedes, and of course the lovely Sian; but he never danced.

Now Julia and I danced; we danced exotically and downright embarrassingly after a few drinks. We liked a lot of room, and always filled it. Sian, she didn't usually dance, and people often thought she didn't like to, but that wasn't strictly true. Being with Ray, the boys didn't tend to ask her, and she wouldn't dance with the other girls, it wasn't her thing. So generally she just didn't.

At Henry's that afternoon Julia and I were, true to form, up and dancing after a few drinks, along with one or two other shameless types. Ray and Sian had been knocking it back too and were singing along with the standards (well Ray was), but they weren't expected on the dance floor. So when Sian leaned across and said "Give us a birthday dance Callum, no chance of getting this old sod up," I was thrown, and on the dance floor was immediately over compensating. It caused some considerable amusement for Julia and Ray as we moved it to The Girl From Iponima. Sian was a great dancer, sexy and lithe, but this contrasted bizarrely with my slightly manic Thunderbirds Are Go routine.

Then there was a slow one and I'd begun to turn away, but a hand firmly gripped my elbow and I was drawn into a clinch. There was an influx of tipsy middle-aged romantics symbolically renewing their vows, and a few younger ones putting down a marker, and I was relieved to be hidden in the crowd. Not that Julia and Ray wouldn't have noticed, but I felt awkward...hand in the cookie jar awkward.

Lost in the mix, like strands of seaweed swaying in a gentle sea, I eased into smooch tempo and relaxed. It felt *so* good. Arms wrapped around each other and Sian's head on my shoulder, I began to drift. With just the slightest inclination of my head I felt her hair against my face, her perfume, her body slowly flexing against mine. It was as if the world had contracted into this slow rhythmical embrace, and I breathed her in, aroused now, awkwardness falling away. This was not the me who had stood up to dance, and she was different too, here, now, close in.

The music pulsed, and we moved together. Her body pressed against mine, her embrace imperceptibly tightening around me. I was aware of her lips soft on my neck and my hand stroking her hair, closer now, her breasts pushing against me, her thighs...and that was not all. My state of arousal was obviously not lost, the barely moving rotation of her hips had found me out and pushed on, insistent, undeterred. I felt her exhale breathlessly against my neck, and entered a state of Nirvana like bliss.

The floor cleared as the music turned up-tempo, and I headed to the bar ostensibly to get another round in, but actually to allow my hard on a few minutes to make its disappearance.

"You make a lovely couple," Ray said as I reappeared with the booze.

"Yeah", I said, "I mean, she's obviously a beginner, but as they used to say, Ginger looked good because of Fred. I thought the girl did good."

Sian offered a patient smile, "Callum, *darling*, I'm just *not* going to dignify it..." I thought I caught a look...perhaps...not quite sure; but either way, things had changed.

The rest of the session was par for the course. A good time was had. Kisses for the girls at the off, and a sharp squeeze on my arm from Sian... it was enough. The cliché would be that we went home and I ravished Julia. Sadly not, though it wasn't for want of a half-hearted attempt on my part, with a refusal that was also fairly par for the course and didn't greatly offend, despite leaving me slightly high and dry, so to speak. I wasn't too bothered. The flesh was unusually keen but the spirit ambivalent. It crossed my mind that Julia probably had a fair idea where the volition came from anyway. She knew I fancied Sian like everyone else. Not that it would have bothered her if she *had* been in the mood...

Chapter 3

Then it was back to the weekly routine. I wouldn't say there wasn't a second thought, because there was…were in fact, quite a few. But the clear light of day has a habit of loading reality on you, however reluctant you are to own it. OK, so it preoccupied me more than it should have done, more than I felt comfortable with, disturbing my self-image as the hard edged realist…the very part of me which countered each and every straying thought with the obvious fact, which that Sian had been mischievous, nothing more, a bit of fun; but then there was the squeeze on the arm. It wouldn't quite go away.

Five a side on Tuesday and drinks with the lads after, then drinks at Sachi and Sachi's on Wednesday. That was Dave and Dave, our gay friends who lived a couple of streets away in a sort of minimalist kitsch splendour. Everyone had called them Sachi & Sachi since time immemorial. Gay men, as everyone knows are typically not camp, but Sachi & Sachi were the exceptions to this rule. They provided Julia and I with a weird and strangely essential antidote to the no kids, professional, heterosexual society, which was, as it had turned out, our thing; baby boomers without babies…mmmmm.

It was Thursday, Julia's Yoga night and she'd just left. I was settling in to watch United-Porto, debating whether to open a bottle of wine. Julia would have just opened one, but I was a prevaricator, the cautious one, with a tendency to indecision. I'd more or less decided I would (open a bottle) when the doorbell rang. Sod it, I wouldn't answer. It rang again, longer and more insistent this time.

I capitulated. It was Sian.

"Sian!"

"Callum."

"Sian!"

"Yes Darling, I think we've already established who I am. Are you going to invite me in?"

I moved aside as she strolled past without waiting for a reply. "Yes of course...sorry...it's just that I wasn't..."

"You didn't know I was coming. I know. That's because I'm calling to see *Julia*, with whom I *did* arrange it...though it is of course *lovely* to see you too!"

"Oh," I said, "She thought you were going to pop round last night...something about a dress? It's Thursday, yoga night, you've just missed her by five minutes."

Sian sat down in the armchair and dropped her bag, crossing her legs (very fetchingly), undeterred if a little perplexed.

"Oh. Damn. It *is* yoga night isn't it; and I was sure we'd said Thursday. Never mind. I can probably help myself if *you* don't mind. It's Jules's white sun dress..."

"Yeah sure. It'll be in the wardrobe. Shall I..."

"Well, actually, I was going to try it on."

It was all above board. Julia *had* mentioned the arrangement. A voice was telling me not to make an idiot of myself, but I was still looking for a hint, hoping for one. She was sitting back in the chair, smiling, waiting for me to say something. Her dress was slightly ridden up showing plenty of bare thigh. I found myself rather too obviously eying her up, but she just sat there, saying nothing, and I looked. Was she waiting for me to make a move? It was flight or fight...I crumbled.

"No...I mean yes...the dress...of course you can. It's..."

"Don't worry…I know where it is Callum," she said quietly, as she rose and crossed to the hall, pausing in the doorway to turn: "I'll… er, I'll not be long."

The football pundits on the TV might just as well have been speaking in tongues. I heard the blood pounding in my ears. I was aroused and it showed, and I suddenly realized that she couldn't have failed to notice.

I tried to focus on the TV but it was useless. Sian was undressing in *my* bedroom, just across the hall! Then her voice drifted to me as if from far away, like a siren calling to Ulysses.

"Callum. Callum…be a love and zip me up would you?"

Surely this was it? I leapt up tripping on the rug in my haste. I was like one of Pavlov's salivating dogs. As I entered the bedroom I saw that Sian was standing with her back to me but slightly sideways on in front of the full length mirror. The fingers of one hand were curling her hair, lips slightly parted, looking at me in the mirror without a word as I approached. Julia's virtually transparent white sun dress hung from her shoulders by flimsy straps. There was a black bra and pants on the bed, and the fabric of the dress clung to her naked body. Her eyes told me…it was all for me.

Yet even now I positioned myself behind her, very close, and felt for the zip. She sighed and closed her eyes, turning her head slightly so her hair brushed against my face. I found the zip but instead ran my fingers lightly up her back and she moaned softly eyes still closed, tilting her head back, her lips there, just there…

"Shit!" she muttered, clipped, like the movie maker "cut," crashing from dream to hard reality as we both heard the sound of car tyres crunching the gravel outside. I stepped back on reflex; caught on the hop. She was looking at me in the mirror and for a very long second there we remained.

"You'd better go Callum," she said quietly. I hesitated and her eyes flashed, "Go...*go!*"

I left the room but left the door half open and turning could still see her, and in the mirror too. I stopped and looked, transfixed, as I heard the car door slam, and watched as she hooked her thumbs under the straps of the dress, letting it fall silently to the floor, footsteps scattering the stones outside...one...two...three...

"Yoga cancelled. What's the score?" Jules came up behind and kissed me on the top of the head.

"Nil nil," I guessed hopefully. "Oh...Sian's here...mixed her nights up. She's gone to try the dress on."

"Oh. Unlike her. Fancy a drink?" And it was...and I did.

"Is that you Jules?" Sian's voice sang out, bright and breezy from the bedroom.

"Yeah...yoga cancelled."

"I'm trying the dress on...got the nights mixed up."

"Yeah, so I hear. Let's have a look then."

"OK...here we go." Footsteps crossing the hall.

When Sian reappeared I initially affected to be engrossed in the football, partly as that's how I normally would have been with the girls doing "girly" things, and partly because I feared I could not look at her without showing something was different...not quite right...something "going on" between us.

"What do you think?"

"Oh Sian it's perfect. Really. Oh it looks much better on you than it does on me. Don't look Callum!"

This was obviously my cue to look, and I was unable to help myself…she looked stunning.

"Oh bloody hell it does!"

"Thank you my love," Jules said in her ever so sweetly voice.

Sian was obviously attempting to write me out of this particular script as she began to consult Julia about whether it was a little this and a little that. I turned back to the football, relieved to be ignored.

After Sian left Julia was uncharacteristically scathing about my remark, and I tried to maintain a healthy disinterest, aided and abetted by the football apparently continuing to hold my full attention.

"Oi…you…there's no need to make it quite so obvious."

"Mmm?"

"I don't mind you fancying her, but there's no need to make it *quite* so obvious."

"I only agreed with you…you usually *like* that!"

"Well it's the exception that proves the bloody rule…and anyway it's not that so much as your eyeballs nearly popping out…I was nearly picking them up off the rug Callum."

It was time for a fight back I realized, defensiveness a sign of weakness and guilt, and Julia had a nose for both.

"But you could see her tits…and even *you* have to admit she has amazing tits. I mean, they *are*! It's just lust darling…I still *love* you (and you alone…etc. etc.)."

"Neanderthal." She swiped me across the head as she passed and I knew I'd successfully appeased her, but she couldn't resist floating in to me the final word from the kitchen:

"Anyway, she's light years out of your league sweety...even *I* only see you as a charitable project!"

"Very funny."

Chapter 4

Over a week had passed since the dress incident, almost two since Henrys. I'd gone over things a thousand times in my mind, swinging wildly betwixt and between like a kid pulling petals off a daisy.

Overall though my hopes were on a downward trend. A bit of flirty dancing, some confusion between Sian and Jules and one of those "situations" with Sian and I. Maybe she *was* up for it…well she was, I knew that for sure, but that was just the way it had worked out. There was a lot of value added by my own over active imagination, stoked by the Peeping Tom image of her nakedness which was burned into my mind. It was a mix up, an opportunistic chance, one that got away. A potential casual fuck with a very gorgeous woman, but that was it…I had to leave it at that and move on. Jules was right; I was window shopping in Knightsbridge with a pocket full of loose change.

I'd seen Ray at footie but neither Julia or I had had seen Sian since, and she hadn't called. I'd resisted the temptation to phone her, and as the days crawled by was relieved that I hadn't made a fool of myself. Yet the naked vision wouldn't go away, and I still found myself tracking back over it all in the wee hours, lying awake. There was something else, something nagging at me that had escaped me. What was it?

Suddenly I was dissatisfied with my lot. I was jolted out of my quiet well-being as if a mosquito had found a way to squeeze itself into my head, flying about in there, settling, flying about again at will with its high pitched whine.

Jules was on my case. Perhaps she could hear the mosquito too. She could sense the subtle shift in our accustomed equilibrium, smell it on my breath. Maybe that's why she was cooking us a posh dinner on the Friday night, looking to get things right again. Maybe that's why I'd found myself scouring the top shelf of the wine bit in Tesco's, looking for something half decent to go with it.

I was sauntering back to the car when I heard a familiar voice.

"Callum…Callum…"

I'd walked past Sian, sitting in her silver BMW, and turned to see her leaning her head out of the window, smiling. Designer shades perched on the top of her head. I retraced the few steps as casually as I could feign, and leant my forearms on the window opening, my face just a few inches from hers. My heard was thudding but I was the essence of cool.

"So this is where you work…sorry darlin' I've only got a couple of quid and seven kids to feed at home…"

"Stop it!" She said quietly, neither joining in the joke or slapping me down with the usual ironic quip. I thought she flushed slightly, something I'd never seen before.

I tried to re-group, searching for something to say, unsure now, my cover blown.

"What about the dress then?" I said. It was one of my less meaningful remarks.

"The dress?" She repeated quietly, looking at me puzzled now, the smile gone, but something else too …expectant…waiting…waiting for me to say something.

Suddenly it hit me…the thing I'd ridiculously missed that had been nagging in the back of my mind for over a week.

"You put it on again," I said at last.

"Oh…yes," she said.

"I saw you take it off…watched you from outside the door…you put it on again."

"I know," she said. "I mean I knew…I knew you were watching…that's why…sorry, I…"

"Don't…don't be…it's me who should be sorry, but I'm not, it was beautiful. I thought…after Henry's… and then in the bedroom…I thought we… I'm going out of my mind Sian."

I dived in; couldn't help myself, sink or swim, it had all been too much. Damn the consequences.

We were looking at each other like strangers, our cosy pals familiarity stripped away. I was there, on the line, waiting for her reply, stopped breathing as if my life depended on it. But she said nothing. She looked away, sighed, began to speak but hesitated. She was searching for words…what words…to tell me to get a grip…move on…that she was shocked, upset? Oh shit. I'd done it now.

"Look…Callum…"

"Watcha me old mate…you propositioning my missus…AGAIN!"

It was Ray.

I straightened up.

"Yeah I was actually, but she says she's stuck being your full time carer… touch of the Clara Schuman to my Brahms."

"Yeah well, you know what they say…one sonata always a nata!"

I had to hand it to Ray. The only thing he knew about Brahms was "Brahms and Liszt", but you just couldn't faze him.

"Anyway," I said, "How do you expect Sian to make a living if you keep appearing every time a bloke sticks his head through her window?"

"Aha, well, I hover invisibly… they seek him here…"

"Would that be the pimp…or Nell?"

"Bubum!"

"Ha bloody ha," came the laconic riposte from the car. Sian had her shades on now and was turning the ignition key, the engine purring into life.

"And if you two have finished your Laurel and Hardy bit I wouldn't mind getting home."

I had to snatch my hand away as the window went up, but not before Ray had finished off with:

"That's another fine mess you've got us into!"

As I drove home I marvelled at this reality we construct for ourselves. There in a truly exposed moment, the veneer swept aside, we had clicked right back into role and saved ourselves by being what was mutually expected. Like a thin layer of colourful petrol on water coalescing once again to mend where a pebble had disturbed the surface and made a hole.

What *had* Sian been going to say? Perhaps I'd never know. I feared the worst. But there was something...*something.* I turned the car into our front, and the crunching gravel conjured up the glimpse of nakedness she had given to me a week ago. A caprice? I thought not, but wondered if the moment had been missed. Yet she had *given* it to me, even though the game was up and Julia about to walk through the door. I had not stolen it as I had thought. It made a difference.

And now more of the same. Julia and I papering over the cracks. Happy families, getting squiffed and maybe having a fuck. Well, why not?

Chapter 5

It was Saturday morning when the call came through on my mobile.

 "Callum...are you able to talk?"

"Yes, Julia's in the shower" I said, lowering my voice nonetheless, sensing immediately what this conversation was about.

"Callum, I haven't much time, listen, can I see you... I mean...oh Callum!"

 My heart was pounding. "Yes...sure...yes ...Sian..."

She cut in as I hesitated, "I'm going to have to go; can you be free tomorrow afternoon?"

"Yes...I mean….yes I'll make sure of it...where?"

"Two o'clock in the lobby of the Clarence...near the airport...do you know it ?"

"Yes."

"Good...see you there….I'll book a room."

"Yes...good...Sian..."

"Got to go...see you tomorrow."

"Yes..." but the line was already dead.

I slumped down on the couch, vaguely aware of my heart still pounding, and took a very deep breath, feeling that I wasn't absorbing the oxygen, taking another breath, head buzzing. How long did I sit there? Julia appeared in the bathrobe towelling her hair, and stopped when she saw me.

"What's up?"

I snapped out of it, "What do you mean, what's up?"

"I mean what's up? Was someone on the phone? What's the matter?"

I still had my phone in my hand. "Oh, nothing. I was just thinking….that was one of the lad's from footie. I said I'd give him a hand moving tomorrow afternoon. I'd forgotten all about it. Bloody nuisance really, could've done without it."

"Why's it a problem? You're not doing anything are you? I hope you're not going to let him down."

Yes! The perfect strike and assisted into the net by the goalkeeper!

"No, I don't suppose so," I said, "Just a pain in the arse that's all. I'll ring him back upstairs….the signal was breaking up again."

It was *so* easy, and I savoured the salty taste of deception on my tongue as I slid away to delete the last incoming number from my call list.

Chapter 6

Two o'clock at the Clarence. Showered, condoms in pocket, heart in mouth. It was one of those modern travel lodge type places near the airport, bright and slightly clinical, and nothing if not anonymous; a good choice. It was quiet in the lobby and I saw Sian immediately sitting over near the lifts looking at the screen of her phone. A kiss for the girl, but on the lips and lingering…

"Let's go up," she said.

 No hesitation as the lift door slid shut, our mouths and bodies collided, urgent passionate kisses, ….short skirt… tanned bare thighs and arse under my hands, tongues sparring, and nails raking down my back. In our room with the door shut we were straight up against the wall just inside the door, devouring each other, my fingers already inside her, wet and inviting, as she fumbled with my zip, wrenching out my cock and snaking a leg around me to impale herself on it as I took her right there, kissing, kissing, her hands gripping my head, nails stabbing into my scalp, as I picked her up bodily and fucked her like a rag doll.

We sank to the floor and fucked our way to the bed, ravenous kisses, clawing , biting, tearing at clothes and grabbing bare flesh, unleashed and wild, rutting like beasts on heat. She was strong and fought to have her way, demanding and submitting by turns, a frenzy of desire, taking each other, this way and that, as we rolled and shunted across the carpet. There was a trail of clothes to the door; at last we were naked but for my shirt dangling from my wrist, my hand stuck in the cuff, and Sian's bra hung around her middle, her knickers torn loose but clinging around one thigh.

Freed from our clothes Sian had taken the initiative, straddling me, and riding me hard, grunting with the exertion as she shagged me, unashamedly pleasuring herself. Her tits bounced mesmerising above me as she rammed down on my dick, hands braced against my chest.

I had never been fucked like this. I felt my spunk begin to rise too soon and tipped her protesting off. "Wait…wait a minute…I don't want to come yet!"

She smiled and lay back, out of breath, reaching out and curling her elegant fingers tight around my throbbing cock. "I'll wait…but I want more…I want it all." She was panting and her voice shook; her eyes were on fire.

Raised on one elbow I took her in, stretched out on the carpet. I traced her curves with my palm, her rounded hips, toned thighs and tummy, her lovely full tits, her neatly manicured v. I touched her face, cupped and stroked her breasts, leant down and lightly kissed each hard protruding nipple. How I wanted her, and marvelled that I had her… naked… here… giving herself to me. I was brim full; I adored her.

"Fuck me Callum," she whispered, "Please…my darling…come in me…make love to me…"

She rose, taking my hand, and I followed. Sian. Sian. She lay on the bed and I paused beside it, her hand still in mine. Her slim supine body was still, eyes closed, like a Picasso drawing. She waited. Her hair was spread dark on the pillow like the contours on a map, her legs together, all of a piece, an angel at rest, but her innocence betrayed by the urgent rise and fall of her breathing. She was waiting for *me*.

Her eyes flickered open, smiling, serene, offering herself, her voice steady and clear: "Take me Callum; have me; I'm yours."

I mounted her. I was at fever pitch, taut like a bow string, but entered her with reverence… with love. The turbulence of passion had spun away like a passing squall, and her eyes held mine as I pushed slowly into her, sliding up into her darkness, sensation opening like a flower, awake, aware like never before. I lay inert, and Sian took my weight, trembling both as I throbbed deep inside her, joined. She held my face, sealing our union with the lightest kiss, the merest brush of lips. It was enough.

How long did we remain so? A moment? An hour? We awakened from our reverie with kisses...more kisses... such kisses, as we began to fuck, slipping into a slow insistent rhythm, fucking effortlessly now in long sweeps of our hips , collisions building, harder, harder, synchronised as one, jarring together ... such sweet hurting... syncopating the pulsing flow of our loving. At last I felt her shudder beneath me, whimper, and begin to orgasm, rolling her head and moaning, crying and calling out for me, crying out and gripping me to her as she bucked and came, moving against me, crying out to me, calling my name. I moved on seamlessly through, and Sian did too, neither missing a beat like jazz musicians hypnotically 'in the groove.' She felt me trembling, taut and on the very brink, and drew her knees up, still thrusting her spread cunt, whispering: "Fuck me, fuck me, fuck me, fuck me...oh...oh...I'm coming....oh god....ohhhhh..!" and with a cry I arched my back, slapping wet and loud against her... again and again and again and again, the air pierced by her cries as I emptied myself into her.

The calm after the storm was total. We both slept, I'm not sure for how long, but I awoke first, Sian's face on the pillow facing mine just a few inches away. In sleep her expression had shed the faint irony, the slight distance that I'd come to know. She looked open, peaceful, childlike almost. She was beautiful. I closed my eyes and opened them again. No, she hadn't disappeared. Her eyes flickered open, and we remained still, just looking.

"Hello", she said at last.

"Hi."

After all that had passed between us, there was yet a touching shyness, a hint of awkwardness which took me back to my youth long ago, and I smiled.

"I feel like I've died and gone to heaven," I said, momentarily forgetting the "treat 'em mean keep 'em keen" philosophy to which I'd always aspired…and failed.

"I think we've just found out what it is to be alive," she whispered.

"Mmmmm…I'd forgotten…no…I never knew! It's never been like this with…" I hesitated, the betrayal of what I had been about to say failing on my tongue.

She wrapped me in her arms, "Shhhh my love, my darling. I have eyes. I know. It's alright. "

"Darling"… not with the usual 'attitude,' but different now; I was doing somersaults inside.

"But you and Ray…?" I must have sounded earnest, incredulous even…well I was, though perhaps strangely not in the slightest insecure; the subject of partners after what had just occurred was merely interesting, academic, a conversation about how life had been before. She laughed in genuine amusement, girlishly putting her hand up to her face as people do.

"Something I said?"

"Callum, Ray and I haven't slept together for two years. He has a 25 year old dancer (how about that one?) over in Cheadle, to whom he beats a path once or twice a week, and who absorbs a fair bit of his fortunately ample disposable income. You don't have to worry about Ray and I."

"Christ!" I said, stunned, but also noticing something else….pleased (what's the apposite phrase….one man's misfortune etc.) "I had no idea….and…I wasn't."

"You weren't what?"

"Worried."

"No."

"...but it's a shock Sian. Bloody hell; I'd thought you two were…"

"Yes I know Callum; you hadn't noticed anything; but of course you wouldn't would you…goes with the territory."

"You've lost me."

The smile, the ever so slightly raised eyebrow: "Callum, you're a man!" Ah, the irony had returned; good, I did rather like it I had to admit. I pondered it all, rolling onto my back as she snuggled into my chest.

"And Henrys…the flat?" I said, stretching back on my pillow, noticing a small crack in the light fitting on the ceiling.

"Oh, I don't know." She murmured. "It just happened. You just… woke me up. I really had forgotten what it felt like. I was…I don't know…I had to follow through, to come to the flat. I couldn't help it. I just wanted to…*had* to have you."

"Well now you have?"

"Yes."

"And…?"

"And …I don't know. I don't know what I expected… but I didn't expect *this*! "

My customary caution had blown far away, but I checked myself none the less, forty not fourteen, though feeling every bit as raw and exposed as in those first childish fumblings where hearts leapt then broke so easily in the new discovery of elation, closely attended by rejection and loss.

I took her in my arms and we kissed. We kissed a lot, long and loving. We made love again slowly, carefully, exploring each other's bodies in wonder; the newness, the different scents, curves and hidden places beneath the hand, the received touch unpredictable and full of daring fresh delights

When it was time to go she trembled in my arms, and when she turned her face up to mine there were tears in her eyes.

"Hey," I whispered, "What's the matter?"

She shook her head and buried her face in my chest, her voice coming to me muffled and small.

"Callum…Callum…I want you so much…"

On the way home I felt the condoms in my pocket and dropped them in a litter bin.

I was ecstatic. I re-ran the film, the unbridled lust, the emotion, the 'connection'; all there…everything, everything I might have dreamed of, had I known how it could be…but I had not known, and was like a stone-age man shown a TV for the first time.

"Make love to me." She had said this. Sian had said this to me. As a pre-pubescent child I had heard Doris Day singing "Move Over Darling" in which these words had featured. Even then, unaware of what sex was, I had picked up on the allure, the come on, realizing somewhere beyond my conscious mind that it referred to something dark and wonderful, wanting and wanton. It had strangely disturbed me, stirred me up, questioning my innocence. Now I knew. Now I understood.

I hummed the tune and scanned the words as I walked; the preceding line: "…and now that I'm no longer free…" and I smiled. So be it…I would give myself up to *this*. I knew that I already had.

Then after came the next line: "The way you sigh, has me waving my conscience goodbye." I was already impervious to any sense of wrong doing, conscience swept away by the tsunami which had crashed into my life; but how damning and prophetic, those words. What would we not do in the name of love?

Chapter 7

Julia and I might easily have been childhood sweethearts, had it not been for the slightly inconvenient fact that her childhood happened in the Stoke potteries, whilst mine was in Manchester. We clicked from the outset when she came up to the Poly Art College at All Saints where I was already in my second year, so it was, if not a school romance, a long-term connection more or less fresh out of school. We both came from working class comprehensive school backgrounds and had similar reference points, which made things easy the 'unsaids,' things that were just understood were always in plentiful supply. It was fertile ground for our quick fire humour and banter which was in itself a sort of intimacy, alongside the other things...the love and sex to name but two. She had style and was her own person and I noticed her straight away. So did a lot of other guys, but she was for me.

The sex was immediate and the love took a little longer. She was 'my type' then...skinny, androgynous almost, but her tits were a decent handful...she was definitely a girl. Spiky cropped blond, Julia looked good with jeans and T shirt without a bra, what I lovingly referred to as "the lesbian look," and one that she kept on over the many years. Not that she was ever a tom boy or in any way other than very feminine. She was eager enough to show it off when the occasion arose, and when she could be bothered. Julia always scrubbed up well.

We were different in fundamental ways, but a good fit and it just seemed to work without too much effort. Perhaps that was a flaw, all too easy and off pat without any mystery, any struggle, the process of really getting to know someone else. Julia was the pragmatist, the practical one, the decision maker, the catalyst. I was the dreamer, toying with Buddhism and the meaning of life, reading the Russians and

Hesse, listening to Miles and being an all-round cool dude. She looked after me. She liked looking after me, and I liked being looked after.

We were inseparable then, which is just as well as we joined the same big company's advertising department and put our art to work to provide us with a living. Actually we did pretty well in comparison to many of our fellow wasters at Art College. The pay was good and got better, and prospects too, which needless to say Julia was the one to take advantage of. I had helped get her in but she soon rose to a managerial position while I treaded water, happy not to have any more responsibility than the lay out in front of me, and keeping my mind focussed on carrying forward the class struggle.

I wasn't up for getting a mortgage and buying a place together, but Julia had the nouse to go ahead and buy a flat off her own bat. We'd lived together on and off and in various combinations with friends through college, and it seemed only sensible that I should move in with her when she bought, though I was quite pissed off when she then stung me for rent; capitalist pig. What a difference that flat made when we got our redundancy packages later on. We were able to scrape together enough for a very nice place in the new refurbished West Didsbury… café society where the beautiful people had settled like butterflies on a buddleia… and now us.

Some of the beautiful people had beautiful children, but quite a lot didn't, so we weren't alone in that respect. It wasn't that we were averse, but there were female problems for Julia that were going to make it nigh on impossible for her to conceive. It just wasn't to be. Somewhere in the recesses we were both sad about it without it being a big thing, and there were compensations for sure.

And then there was Sian. This was something else entirely. I'd known Sian for many years without really knowing her at all. She came from money and had made money. Chic, classy, dry and a tendency to reticence, though conveying plenty in a look or a gesture; none verbals came easily because people always had to look at her; not just men, but women too. She was beautiful, Latin features and lush brunette but it wasn't just that; there was magnetism, a very physical presence over and above her effortless elegance and poise. Sian was an enigma, no less so for having taken up with Ray, a self-made lout from The Smoke; what was that about?

While Julia and I scoured the charity shops Sian would saunter round St Anne's Square or head off to London for a day or two to raid Harvey Nicks. She was a freelance art valuer/consultant, in demand and able to pick and choose her work. She oozed taste, but dressed so that she never looked as if she tried...whatever she wore she wore it well. An occasional smoker of French cigarettes, an exotic hidden tattoo, a small piece of very intimate jewellery, Sian surprised me more than I had ever expected her to. The lovely Sian...great legs, great tits...what can I say? Sian was Sian.

Chapter 8

Life went on. Sian and I managed to meet once or twice a week and stole phone conversations as often as we could. If anything things were better between me and Julia, especially sex. At first I felt guilty. The routine deception was harder to deal with than I had expected it to be, though as time passed I became progressively more inured to it, like any bad habit which you have no intention of breaking. I knew I'd conveniently sold us both short to Sian that first afternoon, and it rankled, that small betrayal. Things hadn't been as bad as all that between Julia and I, and I'd fallen in too easily with Sian's snap dismissal. I had suspended my judgement, worse, put it in hock. That was the start. Perhaps Julia and I *had* drifted into a sort of suburban complacency, a routine taking for granted of our comfortable relationship and comfortable life, but it had been OK; there was contentment, and it had been enough, more than enough, whatever 'enough' is; but then there was Sian.

With Ray things didn't visibly change at all. Any qualms of conscience I felt were at least partly and conveniently salved by the quid pro quo of him having his own bit on the side. Not that Sian was that to me, anything but. I was smitten, distractedly so, the joy of having her marred only by the fact that I could not have her completely, and perhaps I slightly resented Ray for this. A bit rich, but there you go…I was in love and entitled.

She was always going to leave him. We were going to be together, had to be together, this much we quickly acknowledged, but in the meantime she was in his bed every night, and it irked me. On the other hand, Ray was a good mate, and put simply, I was having it away on the side with his woman. I wouldn't have known Sian if it hadn't been for Ray, and probably wouldn't have had a chance with her if he hadn't decided to play away from home and neglect the home fires. Well, the web was fairly tangled all in all. The bottom line was that normal moral considerations just couldn't apply, because I loved Sian and she loved me, and nothing else mattered.

That was how it was. I could live a lie with my best friend and my partner, and even find room for some petty resentment against them for getting in the way of my perfect bliss, because I was in love. I came to understand, eventually, that love not only conquers all, it airbrushes out the nastier bits, what war mongers refer to as 'collateral damage.' Tough for people in the way…those trusting souls who happen to be in the wrong place at the wrong time. It raises the lovers to immunity from sin in all things done in the name of love. Beauty and truth…and the devil take the hindmost.

But what about the main event, the many splendored thing? I'll not try to describe how I felt, what love was like, the veil lifted from the eyes, the agony and the ecstasy. It's been done before and would not be particularly edifying for the repetition. I had never subscribed to a view that great sex and love were necessarily co-dependent, but I'd have to revise that view in respect of Sian. It wasn't that simple. If your only direct experience of cars was to drive the family saloon, you might not necessarily associate driving with exhilaration in speed. I had leapfrogged into formula one, my life flashing before me, dreary and mundane, and here was everything. Not just in the 250mph straights and the breath-taking chicanes, but at rest, replete, and in the ever present anticipation that there was more, endlessly more. It was wonderful. It was bliss. I loved her. I wanted her. I had to have her…at any cost. It was as simple as that. Make love to me…

Chapter 9

It's amazing how easy deception can be. Oh I know that the given wisdom is that you're always found out in the end, and that may be on the whole true, but you can do it for a long time without even being suspected, and perhaps even never found out. It has its own energy and rhythm, and creates its own conditions around it which don't occur in normal circumstances. Some bad things happen, the lies, the betrayals, but there can be unexpected positive spin-offs too, allowing a more benign view, such that you can easily come to believe that you are doing good even by the loved ones who are being duped.

Julia was happier, that's for sure. As I said, our sex improved in both quantity and quality. We tried different things and in different places, and it was altogether more daring and spontaneous than before, more relaxed, more alive. She liked me going out more, and observed that my more energized existence was having a positive effect on me. I was happier and more fun to be around. Of course I had to improvise a stock of standard commitments as well as having a good few spontaneous things which would just crop up when the text or phone call came, but this comes with practice; and when the reason for wanting to get away is as compelling as mine was, you can find yourself practicing very hard...and it does make perfect.

So the deception itself can come to be viewed as all round beneficial, as a source of goodness, or at least of happiness. Already you can see that self-deception too has to be a major part of the process. Not only may you fail to actually acknowledge bad behaviour, to apply any moral standard to it, but far more creatively than that, you construct a chain of logic that not only absolves, but honours you with the elevated status of benefactor, creating the conditions of happiness for all, even those who are abjectly deceived. Not exactly social work, but how can I put it...shagging for the greater good?

The twists and turns of the deceiver's logic and moral disingenuousness could be something to behold. Take for example one sunny Sunday at the height of summer when I was supposed to be taking Julia for a drive up to the Lakes....

Usually weekends were difficult for Sian, but on this particular Sunday she texted me in the morning and I called her.

"Callum, darling can you get away? Ray's had to go into work on some emergency systems failure or something. He's going to be tied up all afternoon. We could head up to the moors....I'll put a skirt on, so long as you don't mind taking me in my boots!" she giggled.

I was going to do it. No question. "Yeah, sure, listen let me ring you back in an hour...just need to sort something out....or I'll text you....or better still just get yourself to the Grapes car park at I-00 and I'll meet you there unless you hear different."

"OK darling...can't wait!"

Of course, she would have waited; she would have called it off if I'd told her about my promise to Julia, but a little sideways deception, just a small omission...somehow I would work it.

"Julia!" I called up the stairs. "JULIA!"

"Bloody hell Callum," (Julia coming down the stairs) "I'm not deaf...what?"

"That was Pete. They've a cup match this afternoon and the goalkeeper's cried off sick...he wants me to stand in....they're desperate..."

"Oh no!" It was the whingey voice, thankfully, not the totally pissed off one, "What about the Lakes? Tell him you can't."

"They're desperate Jules, I'm the last in the list, Christ you know I'm useless in goals, but there's nobody else...and it's a cup match..."

"But I was looking *forward* to it, we both were...*are*! Why do they expect you to give up *your* Sunday afternoon just because *they've* got a problem?"

I sensed the weakness and knew there was a way. "I know. Fuck it I'll tell him I can't!" I began to dial then stopped. "Or..."

"Never mind the 'or', just bloody ring him Callum."

"Just hang on a minute, calm down, I've had a thought. Why don't I do it today, and next weekend we can do the Lakes properly... stay over somewhere Saturday night?"

She paused to consider, and I knew it was in the bag.

"Well it's a bloody pain!" She paused, sighed grumpily, "Ohhhhhh alright then, piss off...it *would* be nice to stay over."

By the time it was time for me to go Julia had quite warmed to the idea and was looking for a cheap deal on the internet when I came down with my football stuff. She put her arms around me and kissed me, rubbing against me.

"Do you have to go right now?" she said in her vamp voice. I kissed her back and squeezed her bum drawing her onto me.

"Mmmmmmm," I said, "'Fraid so," but she was not letting go, kissing me deeply again and again, and muttering accusations in between...

"Are you going out shagging Callum..." "I think you are..." "I think that's what all this is about".... Jules tongue was pushing into my mouth and I was up for it, returning with interest. She was snogging me hard as I blurted out the confession in between:

"OK, you've got me bang to rights…" "It's one of the receptionists from work…" "Lisa…" "You know the little punk one with the big tits…"

Julia was moaning and had her T-shirt up and mine too, pushing her tits against me, voraciously tonguing my mouth.

"Mmmmmmm…you bastard," she murmured unzipping me and pulled out my cock. "What else do you do… you… bastard!" Gasping the last word, as my fingers pushed up her dripping cunt.

"Christ Jules I'm sorry… she likes me to lick her out… and then…" She was pushing me down to the floor.

"Go on what?!Does she fuck you!? Does she!? Like this!? Like…THIS!?" Her skirt was up and knickers yanked aside as she climbed on and slid down hot and wet, fucking me hard right there, on the living room floor. She came quickly and so did I, and she stretched out breathless on top of me, at last giggling and licking the side of my nose.

"Got to go," I said. She purred and didn't move.

"Jules..!"

I shuffled her to the side and she he rose letting me up, but then archly took my hand and shoved my fingers up her again, licking them dry, sultry and theatrical…total vamp: "Save one for me…"

I was cheating, lying, betraying my partner, but the situation readily leant itself to a very benign re-interpretation with just a little bending, a soupcon of creative thinking. I'd managed things so that everyone was happy, much happier than if I hadn't told any lies or changed any plans. So the lies and the changes were not only harmless, but positively beneficial to all concerned.

On the top of Rishworth moor it was, as it were, déjà vu all over again. Right by the trig point, Sian extracting my cock and pushing me to the ground, skirt pulled up, knickers yanked aside…but this was Sian.

Jules was in good spirits when I got home having booked a snip pub B&B deal and made us a great dinner... some old sounds and a bottle of wine, and I fucked her again on the sofa. All of this was positive. Everyone was happy. It worked. By the time I was dozing off to sleep that night I was telling myself that I really had no reason to feel bad at all. Our love, Sian's and mine, was truly a beacon, a source of joy infecting others around us (bad choice of words).

Chapter 10

"You played a blinder tonight my son." Ray sat down with the drinks.

"Yeah, not bad eh? Cheers."

"Dirty weekends must agree with you."

"How did you know about my dirty weekend?"

"Ah, that'd be telling. Julia told me; saw her in Tesco's last week."

"Oh" I said paying some much needed attention to the beer. "Yeah, it was good. Brilliant weather too. Nice old pub we stayed in; Jules got a pretty good deal on it."

"Yeah," Ray said, a little too thoughtfully. "That's not all she told me."

"Oh yeah? Go on then surprise me."

"She said you *were* going to go away the weekend before, for the day, and this was your guilt trip 'cos you had to play in goals for the big boys… in the cup." He sipped his lager nonchalantly.

No, he didn't know. He was fishing. But he knew my football tale wasn't remotely true. Thinking, stalling…

"Yeah? What do *you* think?"

"*I* think, young man, that you have *not* been playing the beautiful game, but you *have* been playing away from home."

"Cheers" I said, taking another long and leisurely sip. "I've got a bad feeling about Stamford Bridge on Saturday."

"You dirty little sod, you have haven't you?"

I capitulated, conspiratorial…lads talk…

"Yeah alright, just a bit….but you keep it under your fucking hat!"

"You lucky bastard; go on spill."

I was starting to enjoy it.

"Yeah, lucky is the word. She was just there, gorgeous, unloading her shopping. A bag ripped and it was all over the pavement…"

"So you had to help…"

"Well yeah. Very grateful… invited in for a coffee… kids at school, husband away…."

"You lucky bastard."

"You've already said that Ray." I was grinning very broadly now, "My round," and off to let him wait for the next bit.

"Cheers. "

"Cheers."

"Anyway, it gets better…."

"Oh no, do I want to hear this….?"

"Her husband works away a lot, and she's really up for it, I mean, she *really* does it Ray, I mean REALLY does it."

"Oh no! It just isn't right!"

"AND. She likes to play a bit, you know, the lingerie and the visuals and all that."

Ray's East End accent was coming through stronger now.

"Oh fucking hell Callum leave it out… you're making that up!"

I sipped my pint smugly…a sigh and a faraway look. "Lovely jubbly," I said; game, set and match.

The thing was, I could very easily have been talking about Sian, who I had discovered to my great joy had a definite penchant for the 'visuals' verging (much to my delight) on downright exhibitionism. Anyway, Ray kept his own indiscretions to himself, which really I was quite glad about. He even gave me some 'Be careful' advice…nothing if not rich. Oh what a tangled web…

Chapter 11

The weekend in the Lakes with Julia *had* been good. Not exactly Cordoba, and I knew by then that we would never go to Cordoba together, but those were 'in the moment' times. It didn't do to think too much. Julia was very sweet and we got on very well, notching up Scafell Pike, and finding a tiny valley off the path where we stripped naked in the sun and fucked each other on the sheep cropped turf, Julia on top. She looked lean and athletic and she rode me hard so I felt taken. She was having her way, taking her pleasure, and I was excited by it, inciting her to do me, and she responding like a horse urged over the jumps, bucking ferociously as she pinned my arms to the turf. Not quite the Ferrari I'd become accustomed to but a nice little runabout...I wasn't complaining. It was risky... May in the National Park, but that added a frisson and the climax was tempestuous as we came together recklessly loud, then scrabbling round in a giggling panic for our clothes, suddenly afeared we'd be spotted!

We stayed at The Queens Head at Troutbeck in the middle of nowhere. It was surprisingly cool in the old pub and they still had a log fire going in the inglenook. Climbers and a few couples knocking back the beer and a fair bit of chat and banter as the night went on, then back to Julia's rules (for that night) sex: she was in charge...black suspenders and stockings...the lot, and every whim to be obeyed. A year before it could never have happened and if it had would never have worked; but here we were... a revelation.

We talked about staying for another night, but the lack of funds intervened and we headed back on the Sunday as planned. Things were a lot better between Julia and I. It made it much easier as time went on to mitigate the urgency that I at first felt to set up with Sian. Sian seemed happy to be coasting too. Life was good.

It was all so easy. Sex with Julia had become fun and exciting; but with Sian it was everything, from the animal to the sublime and a rainbow of colours in between, a treasure trove of delights. It was a gift and at once an art, which she had cultivated, honed to perfection. Julia I viewed as a fond friend who I shagged, who liked being shagged, so that was OK; but to Sian I was in thrall. She was my beautiful accomplished teacher, and I the avid student. I adored her.

Sian and Ray came to ours, we went to theirs, and we all reciprocated with Sachi & Sachi too. Other parties and small gatherings, trips to the pub, the usual socializing dotted along the way. Overall Sian and I were impeccably behaved, apart from one very quick and ridiculously risky fuck in a disused attic, at a party in a large rambling house on Palatine road. Ray and Julia were downstairs oblivious…it seemed a good idea at the time… Sian's I hasten to add. We were quite smug at how well we carried it all off, and it did mean that we saw each other socially…which made a nice change…

Chapter 12

Then came the next Sunday session at Henry's. It was the beginning of August, and the occasion was Dave's (Sachi and Sachi) birthday, so we were doing the traditional Sunday afternoon thing. The Dave's were always great fun, extrovert and over the top. It was impossible not to have a good time. Being a party pooper was not allowed. They were up dancing dragging Julia and I with them even before we had had what we would have deemed to be our pre-dance quota of drinks, which meant that we were probably over compensating and hamming it up even more than usual. Sian was not so easily swayed and had demurred, and Ray…well Ray doesn't dance.

It was hectic and hot, and when we sat down we were topping up with a vengeance. The Daves wouldn't let us rest for long. Birthday Dave had squeeze in between Sian and Ray, and was mercilessly teasing Ray.

"Are you not going to dance with me Raymond… just one teensy weensy little dance for my birthday?"

"Yeah go on Ray," I chimed in, "Nobody'll think you've turned *darling*…we'll get Sian up too…she can be your alibi!"

"Oi, leave it out stirrer. Anyway I want *you* up dancing with Sian again; the last time you two hit the floor she had me up half the night!"

Sian was cool as ice with the stock reply "Huh, in your dreams Raymond."

I was looking at her, stunned trying not to be, trying to think of something witty and light to say, but the words wouldn't come. I thought she shook her head almost imperceptibly, telling me it wasn't true. Meanwhile Ray was on a roll.

"Oh dear, was that a cock I heard crowing?"

"Oooooooh, don't bring cocks into it darling" Dave interjected stroking Ray's thigh, "You're getting me all of a fluster!"

The general hilarity was lucky. I felt as if the blood had drained from my face, and picked up my pint to hide behind for a moment at least whilst I gathered myself.

It passed, the Daves now in tandem teasing Ray, and Julia trying to get a snap of it on her mobile. I glanced again at Sian and caught her eye…another barely visible shake of the head. Julia turned to say something to me but stopped short.

"Callum, are you alright? You look awful."

This was my cue and I grabbed it. "Yeah, don't know, just come over really sick all of a sudden. I'll nip out for some air…might have to take myself off."

"I'll come with you," she said, "We're just going outside for a minute."

I made my escape with solicitous expressions of concern from Ray and the boys, and Sian looking on helpless. Of course I never went back in and asked Julia to apologize for my early departure, blamed the prawn curry take away from the night before, and made my escape.

I walked aimlessly. The numbness blocked everything at first, unable to think, sunk in a hole, fearful of peering over the edge… seeing what was there. It was like walking off cramp, focussed on that one thing and unable to contemplate anything beyond it; but when cramp goes its better. Now as the numbness wore off the hurting kicked in. Doubt had entered my world like a wraith. What I had held to be perfection had a hairline crack, a flaw, but one that drew the eye, filled it.

Sian had lied. There was no doubt about this. I knew it. I saw again that movement of the head, the denial, but Ray's second remark had sealed it… and the cock crew. He wasn't bluffing. If only she hadn't said it…she had no need to tell me that she and Ray didn't sleep together. It was a concoction, an embellishment…why? To soften me up, a barb hidden in the bait to reel me in? How much of the rest was untrue? What about the dancer? Did she exist at all, and if she did, was she just the bit on the side for Ray? Was I her counterpart for Sian, a bit of spice, what's good for the goose and all that… and all that. The crack travelled, branched and spread as doubts invaded me. She didn't love me. If she loved me she would not have lied.

My phone rang. It was Sian. I let it ring, but it was so hard to stop myself from answering. What could she say; what could I say? Oh I wanted to hear her voice, for her to tell me everything was alright, to have her rush to me and take me in her arms; but what then? Trust had escaped Pandora's Box, dragging hope in its slipstream. I was in despair.

There was a message on my voicemail; Sian.

"Callum, Callum, listen, it's not true…Callum, darling, it's **not true**. I've got to go back in. I'll get away. I'll phone you. Please don't shut me out. I love you…I can't bear it…" it tailed off in sobs.

How could such despair turn on a sixpence? I felt a steadying floor beneath my feet, and a glimmer of light in my darkness. What kind of sorcery was this? If I was a fool right then, I was a willing fool, wanting things to be as I had just moments before seen clearly that they were not. Or had I then been a hapless victim of my own base corrosive doubt, tarnishing our perfection with my weakness, my lack of faith, stalling at the faintest breath of a headwind, betraying our love?

I sat on a low wall and felt my breath begin to even out, and some of the tension seep out of my chest. I had to see her. She would ring again, soon, and we would arrange to meet. I mustn't go home. Julia might cry off and go home to see how I am. Just sit tight and wait; walk a bit more; yes, better to move, keep moving, don't think. I got up and walked.

My phone… Sian…I picked up without looking ."Hi."

"Callum…where are you." It was Julia…damn.

"Oh. Hi…I'm…in the park."

"In the park? Callum you sound odd, are you alright? I nipped home to see how you are…I was worried about you."

"Oh, I'm sorry Jules, you shouldn't have; I don't want to spoil your day too."

"Don't be silly, I can be back at Henry's in five minutes. But I'm *worried* about you. How are you feeling? Why didn't you come home?"

"I did… but then… I just felt sick again and thought it had been a bit better out in the air. I'm just sitting on a bench in the park. Feel like an old geezer. Don't worry, you go back and have some fun."

"I'm not so sure about the fun darling, Sian's looking like death warmed up now….anyway I'll go back if you're sure, I'll walk through the park on the way and sooth your fevered brow, where exactly are you sitting?"

"No don't Jules, I'm better just sitting by myself for a bit, honestly, it'd be really nice but I'm just best left to myself."

"OK darling, but promise you'll ring me if you get worse, it could be food poisoning and that can be really nasty."

"Yeah, don't worry….it's not…I'm sure it's not…and I will. You have fun. Give my love to the gang."

Standing in the street, phone still in my hand ; nothing clever about any of that, shamelessly spinning to the one person who I knew genuinely cared about me . A wave of self-disgust swept over me.

I don't remember sitting down on the bench at the memorial green. I must have dozed off, some sort of physical cut out mechanism no doubt when there is a temporary mental disconnect occurring. Disorientated, a group of passing teenage girls giggling, and I realized my mobile was ringing…Sian…I fumbled in my pocket. "Hello."

"Callum, Callum it's me. I've got the car I'll pick you up…darling please…don't say no…where are you?"

I hesitated and looked around me.

"Callum…*Callum*…"

"Yes…yes…sorry I was looking to see where I am."

"Oh Callum. Where *are* you!?"

"I'm sitting on a bench at the memorial green." She was on her way.

I saw her silver BMW approaching and stood up. I felt awkward and exposed, but this evaporated as I climbed into the car. The familiar navy upholstery, Sian's perfume, the comforting purr of the powerful engine idling, waiting for direction. She took me in her arms, and I clung to her.

No words and she drove. A quiet lane near Gatley; she parked up on the verge…it would do.

"I haven't got much time. Callum it's not true, you must believe that. He was bullshitting." She was calm now, earnest, holding my hand, looking steadily into my eyes.

"It sounded true Sian," was all I could muster, a wan smile playing round my mouth, apologetic almost. "Why would he say it if it wasn't true?"

She squeezed my hand held in both of hers.

"Callum you don't understand, you think you know Ray but you don't. He's an operator. He hasn't got a scrap of paper to his name but look where he's got too…doesn't that tell you something? Callum Ray isn't one of the pearly kings and queens."

"You've lost me Sian. So Ray's climbed the greasy pole standing on a few hands and shoulders, is that it? But what's that to do with any of this? I don't get it."

"No. OK, OK, I'll spell it out. Ray's been slightly smarting since your revelation about your affair with the shopping woman. I could see it straight away…you must have seen it too, I bet he was jealous as hell wasn't he?"

"Well yes, I suppose he was…"

"And he saw a chance to score a point, to get one-up…it's as simple as that…it's instinct to Ray…he's an operator, it's what he does Callum."

"But he has the dancer," I said "That's us even isn't it? Why would he need to do this?"

Sian laughed, a dry bitter laugh.

"Oh Callum, you're such an innocent. Don't you get it? Rays whole life has been getting one up…evens doesn't hack it, not for Ray. Anyway he doesn't know you know about her…and he *does* know you fancy me!"

I pondered it, convinced now that I'd been wrong, a heavy sigh escaping as I took Sian's hands in mine. She looked steadily at me.

"Do you think I'd have said what I did if it wasn't true my darling? Why would I have done that?" She had turned my own logic completely around, her voice breaking up now and tears were welling up and spilling. "I love you, I love you, oh god I can't bear it!"

She shuddered with pent up emotion and bowed her head exhausted, shoulders shaking with her sobs as she let go. I gathered her into my arms and held her.

Chapter 13

West Didsbury was a kind of rags to riches story in the space of twenty years. Several long leafy roads of large dilapidated Victorian houses ran off Lapwing Lane, bounded by Burton Rd and Palatine Rd. They were referred to as 'bed-sit land' in my student days, similar to parts of Whalley Range. If not quite a case of faded grandeur, you could easily see that these were substantial examples of Victorian suburbia which had known much better times. Back then they had been tackily converted to house the maximum number of low rent-payers. These would typically be students, but also a plethora of the lonely, the misfits, the flotsam and jetsam of society, eking out their lives here in one room, and beating a path to the Midland hotel on pay day.

As a student I had a bed-sit on the first floor at 26 Clyde Rd. It was very different back then. There was a drug dealer in the front bedsit, and an African medical student in between mine and his. Underneath me lived a big red faced Irish navvy who used to bounce around his room singing 'Long haired lover from Liverpool' when drunk once or twice a week. Downstairs at the front there lived a strange middle aged chap, a stick of a man, who's ritual each time he left the building was to face the mirror in the hall, hands in prayer position, and mutter in a high pitched 'Goons' voice before striding out purposefully and slamming the front door. Once I glance through his open door a barely furnished room dominated by a huge pile of what appeared to be toffee papers in the middle of the floor. All life was there.

There was a similar if slightly better area to the north of Lapwing lane, and more modern housing too, spreading up toward Withington where there was the mandatory council estate. The usual shops, takeaways, and pubs clustered around the junction of Burton Rd and Lapwing Lane. Within less than a generation however it changed beyond recognition.

The Victorian houses were at last bought up and refurbished for both up market rentals and private ownership. The pubs, shops, takeaways, everything was prettified and converted to cater for what I have referred to as 'Café Society,' and drew in visitors from round and about whilst the locality atmosphere and amenities for the local people suffered. The once very ordinary local, the redbrick Midland Hotel, became 'The Met,' a trendy place with bouncers and cocktails, packed most evenings to bursting point with young people. The tiny Railway across the road was unrecognisable from the spit and sawdust Marston's drinking den of old.

This was where Julia and I and many of our friends now lived, a manicured and manufactured suburb for the would-be nouveau something. Well, I am exaggerating a little perhaps, but not that much; and if I have made it sound shallow and somewhat inauthentic I don't apologize for it. For all its faults though it had some innate character, and was an easy and pleasant place to live for middle aged middle class professionals like ourselves. We liked it, as well as being suitably deprecating about it when the occasion required. As the late Kenny Everet used to say, "...and of course it was all done in the best *possible* taste!"

Chapter 14

The incident at Henry's, perhaps a blip in one sense, was traumatic. Our complicated and dishonest living situation was shown to be vulnerable and not sustainable. My behaviour toward Julia bothered me… dissembling, lying to her as she had expressed her concerns and tried to support and comfort me. I was beginning to dislike myself. I vowed that nothing like this should be allowed to happen again, but did nothing to insure against it or to move the situation on.

Sian once more filled my vision. The awfulness of the tremor for both of us caused a rebound to each other. Whatever doubts had for me arisen were buried deep and out of sight. Sian was even more loving and attentive. Our sex exploded to new heights of passion and tenderness, and Julia and I were fucking along in the slipstream. Julia remarked on it, and if I felt a twinge of guilt I was also guilty of encouraging her, enjoying her, feeling good too.

I had my cake and ate it. It was the behaviour and the logic of the addict; shades of Macbeth: "Stars hide your fires, let not light see my black and deep desires, the eye wink at the hand." Perhaps I wasn't just quite as magnificent as he was, but I could be every bit as me, me, me! I was having trouble sleeping and acquired a prescription for pills to assist.

So things carried on much as they had before, with perhaps an additional frisson resulting from the awareness of danger and fragility. The Henry's incident had burned us. I talked to Sian in the immediate aftermath about the need to bring things to a head, to dissolve our respective commitments and be together, but she wanted more time. Her intuition was that Ray was moving toward a denouement with the dancer, which would make things far easier for us to set up together. I had to agree. The prospect of a major head to head with Ray was not one that I relished. Such talk faltered, stopped, and found its way to the proverbial back burner.

We found ourselves looking toward Christmas, and as time went by things between Julia and I were becoming more difficult. There was no movement with Ray, and it took a lot of energy maintaining the deception in order to grab what increasingly felt to me to be scraps of a life with Sian. I was no longer energized and a 'Master of the universe.' Julia was less accommodating about my coming and going, and we both became quite tense and irritable. I still found a real thrill in taking her, in having her as well as Sian, sometimes on the same day, but Julia's keenness to be taken diminished as the weeks passed. She liked the fucking and often gave in just because she wanted the sex, but she was fed up with me; she was annoyed when my extra mural activities interfered with things at home or impinged on things we were supposed to be doing, but otherwise she was less and less bothered or interested in what I did.

She made a bid to interest me in going with her to Tango classes, which we'd talked about in the past, but I resisted guarding my time for Sian. I was unable to come up with any good reason other than that I didn't feel like doing it, and this led to a row, which was quite unusual for Julia and I. She was exasperated and very angry, what was the matter with me, I had "changed." She subscribed to go by herself.

Julia was in the jobs market and looking to get out of her rut, and it was just a matter of time before she found something. She was bright and good at what she did. My fumbling dissembling distraction was thrown into sharp relief against her energised focus, and it could only get worse. I saw it, but simultaneously failed to see it. I was banking on a future with Sian, and maintaining my comfort zone in the meantime whilst putting little in, and the nagging buried doubts whispered in the shadows.

Julia, Sian, Ray, all had lives that looked outward, had substance, were somehow *real,* whilst mine was contracting and I felt the walls closing in. One thing only filled my thoughts, increasingly the addict, hooked on the rush, the gambler; but each time I was with Sian, every time I held her made love to her, I was sustained, reinforced in the knowledge that this prize was singular and worth everything. It would be mine. All would be well.

Chapter 15

Whilst life for me stumbled along in a state of inertia, Julia didn't stand still. She had a telephone call from a friend of ours at the old firm. Someone had left, leaving a plum job, assistant divisional marketing manager for the north-west. It had Julia's name written all over it. She was well thought of there, and within a fortnight it was wrapped up, company car, the lot. It was a real coup, and Julia was up for it, smart power dressing suit and heels appearing after a girls shopping expedition with Sian. I took the piss no end, but had to admit, she looked pretty good.

It was good news all round. Sian organised her own working week and anyway seldom put in a full five days, and this freed me up during Julia's working hours. The money would be welcome too. With the summer behind us Sian and I were entirely dependent on the use of hotels, and I had felt bad about Sian generally footing the bill, so I saw the prospect of being in a position to pay my way...or at least for Julia to do so. Mercenary, shameless, yes I was those things, but I was able to block any inconvenient moral scruples; only one thing mattered.

Sian fully preoccupied me. Everything referred back to this. Everything and everyone existed in the long shadow cast by our love. It was my raison d'etre. It was akin to the cuckoo in the nest that had to be fed. I had to feed it, slavishly, compulsively, only able to see this one thing, this beak that opened wide, stimulating my response. Only for me it was Sians's legs...and no I'm not being flippant...that's how it was. What would have been out of bounds, a step too far? It's scary to think of what I might have been capable. Where would I have drawn a line, or was John the Baptist always going to lose his head?

The nature of the love affair is that you have very limited time together, and that time usually focuses on sex. You have to be careful about being seen out and about together. Opportunities to spend more leisurely relaxed time together away somewhere seldom arise. Perhaps if it were not for the snatched and precious minutes together, and the perceived risks always lurking in the clandestine, the excitement would not be sufficient to sustain it for long; the novelty of the new naked plaything would more quickly wear off.

Often love affairs are really sex affairs, even the ones where love is declared and believed in, to all intents and purposes true. The affair is sustained in secret, even in serious adversity and at great risk, by the precious intensity of the drip-fed sex, time and opportunity rationed, and succumbing to the eternal law of supply and demand.

For Sian and I the connection was more than that, much more. Well I *would* say that, but as the saying goes, it's for me to know. Sex was at the core, but the depth and intensity of our sex together was a connection of such consuming intimacy. We mated, coupling like wild animals, we lingered in sublime tenderness. There were games (and toys) and she paraded and teased, stripping and performing uninhibited sexual acts for me, appetizers before fucking. Fucking; fucking with Sian was not one thing but an endless array of possibilities, though always in the final climax and orgasm was something singular and special, a union of being which overwhelmed us, possessed us, abandoned to and in each other; there are no words. Was it love? What is love? We thought it was. For me it was worth everything. It became everything; 'everything'; there it is again.

I said Julia's job was good news all round, and it surely was. She travelled around the region and sometimes to London and Edinburgh, overnights away being not uncommon. She was in good fettle, and the reduced time we had together was better for a while, though that close connection, that vital spark of mutual understanding and ready repartee had slipped. How can I put it, it was all a bit more 'measured.' Julia had a lot on her plate and maybe just didn't have either the time or inclination to concern herself about me, and in any case having me there as a house husband was actually quite handy, and in that respect I kept my end up. The money made a big difference and we were able to eat out more and get away for short breaks in posh hotels. After her initial splurge on work clothes Julia's wardrobe continued to upgrade and expand. Chic and feminine became the order of the day, and she wore it well, dressing with an idiosyncratic edge and turning a head or two when we were out on the town. I liked it, and she knew.

Sex was on the up again too, and I found myself fancying her something rotten, but it was different now, and more on Julia's terms. She had always had a sense of the theatrical, and her latent tendencies toward the vamp, not to say the high class tart, found expression in a new and audacious line in lingerie, and a penchant to tease and dominate, to be in charge. She'd done it before, but more tongue in cheek, a game after a few drinks. With hindsight I've wondered if it may not have been all such innocent fun, whether the sexual domination game and my mock subjugation may have given Julia a symbolic retaliatory buzz, maybe some catharsis in there somewhere.

Julia's star was in the ascendant, and I enjoyed the fringe benefits, without perhaps fully appreciating the tidal drift and the implications of the subtly changing balance of power. I didn't think about it. I was like a pig in shit, taking what was on offer from the two women in my life, keeping house and keeping them both happy, and myself happy too, possessor of the proverbial bun *and* the halfpenny. Did I really believe this? Well, probably not.

Chapter 16

It was November and I was restless. Julia being in work now left me home alone and often at a loose end. Dark mornings and afternoons didn't help, prone as I always was to the SADS. I tended to drift round to the Sachis where Dave was the perfect housewife and entertained me with the shake and vac, as well as providing me with endless cups of coffee and the occasional lunch.

Dave was a lovely guy, as was Dave 2, and I found myself envying their happy uncomplicated domestic bliss. All those religious bigots who argue endlessly about gay marriage should pop round to the Sachis. How badly we, their heterosexual friends, managed our lives and relationships by comparison, in our allegedly 'natural' pairings as intended by god. The Adam and Eve factor was as relevant as ever, serpents and all.

I felt the need to talk to someone about my situation, and was tempted to unburden myself to Dave, but thought better of it. I could trust him of course, but the idea of him being tainted even by just knowing about the sordid goings on among his friends didn't sit well. Then again, though I didn't expect that he would be accusatory or judgemental, he may well, just on the basis of ordinary morality and common sense say things that I would not particularly want to hear, even though I knew them already.

"So how does it feel being a kept man darling….hah listen to me, and me as kept as they come!"

"Oh it's OK Dave…the money's making life easier. We were struggling a bit before."

"Yes I'm sure, but you must be missing our little Julia, and her a big boss person now! I saw her the other day in the paper shop in her suit and heels…..ohhhhh and those tights with the seam up the back….nearly made me want to turn!" The good thing about conversations with Dave was that they weren't very demanding on you to make a contribution.

"But it would be nice if you got something too Callum. You're bored aren't you, plain as the buttons on my fly...well, studs now...ooooooh, studs...can't' live with 'em and can't live without them! Which reminds me, my young man said he saw you and Sian the other day. You could do something arty like Sian. You've got an art degree haven't you? There you are then! That girl makes a mint, and I don't think she does very much."

"Yeah; Dave, keep that under your hat will you? She was after buying a leather jacket for Ray and I'm the same size...I think it's meant to be a surprise."

"Worry not petal, my lips are sealed, and Dave's will be too. Ooooooooooooh, my Dave's lips! Do you know, even after all these years he still sets me all a tremble! Oh but Julia with those posh outfits...bet you're like a pig in muck...snuffling for truffles half the time I have no doubt. Oh listen to me... sorry sweety it's a cess pit! Well you know it's a cess pit!"

Dave's housewife of the year must have inspired me. It was Thursday, five a side night, and as I returned home I was already planning to make a nice dinner for Julia. I'd picked up a vintage Rioja on the way, and a bottle of Chablis which I deposited in the fridge. I'd done the weekly supermarket shop in the morning, so we were well stocked with fresh food. If I cooked in the afternoon we could eat mid-evening after footie. I was feeling quite perked up. I liked cooking, and actually wasn't bad. In fact Dave didn't have the monopoly on the housewifery arts, as my shopping cooking and cleaning would attest. In a passable Dave impersonation I mused aloud to myself about ("Ooooooooh...") working my fingers to the bone.

Another coffee first though. I pondered Dave's assessment of Sian's business...lots of reward for limited exertion, and I did have an honours degree in fine art. I toyed idly with the fantasy of Sian and I running a lucrative business as a partnership. Finding gainful employment had slipped off my agenda some time ago, and being an unfaithful house husband was a demanding enough occupation for now; but the fantasy appealed...we could be together all the time.

I'd no sooner reached for a couple of cook books when my phone rang. For an instant I dared to hope it might be Sian unexpectedly free, and in that split second was already cancelling the meal. It was Julia. She was ringing to say something had come up at work and she was going to have to shoot off down to London, possibly to stay over the weekend.

She came home to pack a bag. I was irritated at being abandoned and humphed around as she busied herself finding the things she needed. She was gone. The weekend loomed suddenly large and empty, and the cook books were returned to the shelf.

Chapter 17

Football was a tonic. I'd worked hard and though we lost had been pleased with my game. I'd shaken off the torpor of the afternoon. Ray was in a good mood too, heading off with Sian later for a posh Italian. I comforted myself with the knowledge that the ice cream would be the only afters he would be getting. It was a mean thought.

The beer was always at its best after footie or the gym, and we savoured it contentedly. Freda Payne's "Band of Gold" was playing, whisking me back to college days. We played down in Sale, and if the lads weren't going en masse to the cavernous Royal Oak around the corner, Ray and I usually stopped off here at the Bull in Northenden. It was a small Robinsons pub, one of the rarities that had been done up to make it comfortable without ripping out the soul of the place. Most of the original hardwood remained, and the mirrors behind the optics, even the old flag floor in the vault.

That was one of the things I liked about Ray…he didn't have to chat, to fill the silence. Perhaps the song held memories for him too. I suddenly longed for the curl of cigarette smoke, though I hadn't had one in years.

"Penny for 'em," Ray said.

"Oh it was just taking me back…Freda Payne, and funnily enough I was suddenly fancying a fag."

"Yeah. Not the same is it, without smoke…the atmosphere…quite literally as it happens."

"Yeah."

"What you up to then, the man of leisure?"

"Oh don't you start; I've already had Dave going on at me about being a kept man."

Ray laughed, easily able to picture the conversation.

"I don't know Ray, Dave's right, I am a bit bored. There's nothing much out there in my line. I was thinking of picking Sian's brains about what she does…looks like money for old rope to me."

Ray mulled it for a moment. As I'd anticipated, he would genuinely want to say something constructive and to be of help. He wasn't jumping in though, thinking before he spoke.

"Forget it Callum old son, you wouldn't hack it. It's a real jungle where Sian operates. I mean it really is…you'd be amazed. All that haut couture and high flown arty stuff, and it's dog eat dog, ….no place for innocents mate; you wouldn't last a day."

Innocent…me! When had I last been called an innocent? Actually I had, but it didn't immediately come to me. "Leave it out Ray, it's arty farty nonsense isn't it, and Sian's not exactly one of the Kray Twins." Ray had his knowing smile, and again sipped his lager thoughtfully.

"I'll tell you what Callum, you're a good mate, and I wouldn't say this to anyone else. Sian and I've been together a long time, and it works. Why does it work…because we understand each other. First rule of love and war…know your enemy! Sian's an operator, she's a player…charm the birds out of the trees. She'd convince you that black was white, and you'd want it to be white! That's the business she's in, and she's good. Stick to what you know old son. Anyway, what's the worry if Julia's raking it in again? Something'll come up."

I remembered then of course where I'd last been told I was an innocent, along with the other things Ray said about Sian, though from her lips about him. I was confused. I felt the doubt that I had long ago buried worming around like a maggot in my entrails. Ray was still smiling, warmly, not a trace of irony; the smile of a friend. That was a lot for Ray to say at one go, and not just the quantity. He was letting me into his life, but I wished he hadn't. I was floundering, wanting him to somehow change what he had said, say it wasn't true.

"Sian? Come of it Ray. Who's the operator? Of you two it'd have to be you. Sian…Sian's just…"

Ray interjected finishing the sentence for me,

"Yeah yeah…Sian's just the lovely Sian!? Well I'll tell you what old son, you right. I didn't get out of the east end by sitting on my hands and watching my p's and q's. Oh but I watched alright…looked, listened, learned. The thing is, it takes one to know one, and I've probably taught Sian everything she didn't already know; but believe you me, that wasn't vey bloody much. You for another?"

Chapter 18

I got Ray to drop me at the Indian on the way home and picked up a takeaway. He was being really nice, and had suggested I should come over at the weekend for dinner if Julia didn't make it home, or come anyway and bring her if she did. He must have picked up the fall off in my mood, but probably put it down to Julia's heading off and me being stuck on my own.

The Rioja was too good to have with a curry really, but what the hell. What the hell indeed. Suddenly I was very tired; weary tired. I was like a marionette, pulled this way or that depending who had hold of my strings. I ate and drank absently, playing and replaying the conversation with Ray in my mind, and then the one I'd had with Sian in the car that time. The content was so uncannily similar in many respects, but the meaning crucially different. I thought about how I'd felt after leaving Henry's, sure that Ray's comments had been sincere and true; then what he had said tonight:

"….she could convince you that black was white, and you'd *want* to believe that it was white."

Here I was again, knowing, *knowing* that Ray had been speaking his mind, but not wanting to believe it.

The plate was only half empty and half the wine gone already. I poured another glass and went to sit in front of the blank TV screen.

The other thing that had struck me, that I had been unable not to notice, was that underlying what might have been construed as quite a critical assessment, Ray had alluded with affection to a deep understanding with Sian, a real connection, something special, and it was perhaps this that unsettled me more than anything else. This didn't seem to be a man who was treading water in a convenience relationship for which he had no true regard.

But then I thought about Sian, about how she was with me that night, utterly convincing, distraught, bereft, and it all changed again.

By the time the Chablis came out of the fridge I was beginning to see the funny side, torn between my best friend and my (his) woman, and before too much longer rediscovering Buddhist philosophy and reflecting on the elusiveness of truth. By the time the whiskey came out I was furious, to hell with her, to hell with them both. And by the time I fell into my empty bed, silent tears bled me into sleep.

I was awakened by the phone. It was Julia.

"Hello darling, just a quickie. Look I'm really sorry but I am going to be stuck down here till Monday. The big boss wants me at a meeting. Hello? Callum?"

"Yeah...yeah...sorry Jules, just woke up...bad night and I must have slept in. What time is it?"

"Eleven. What's the matter, are you ill?"

"No...nothing just couldn't sleep. How's it going? When do you think you'll be home?"

"Oh I'll be away by lunchtime so it'll be late afternoon...you can make us something nice for dinner and we'll have that nice bottle of Rioja you sneaked in yesterday, if you haven't guzzled it already that is."

"You don't miss much. Drank it last night actually, and the Chablis that was in the fridge...the one you didn't notice."

"Well I wouldn't put it past you!"

Despite my aching head I couldn't help a smile; when I did tell the truth for once she didn't believe me.

"Listen, Jules..." I tailed off, not knowing what I wanted to say, wanting to say something, wanting her there with me.

"Callum? What? Listen you have the Rioja with something nice tonight...treat yourself. We'll get some more on Monday."

"Yeah, sure, I might just do that. Listen, you take it easy, and don't be driving like a maniac coming home." That was that.

A mug of tea, and starting to feel vaguely human though no less sorry for myself, when the phone rang again.

"Hello, Callum darling, it's Sian."

It was the slightly theatrical "darling" that told me Ray was there.

"Hi Sian, what's happening?"

"Well Raymond here instructed me to phone you (because being a man he isn't able to use the phone himself). He said you may be on your lonesome and he's invited you around for dinner."

"Oh, yeah, he did mention it. How was your Italian?"

"Oh, nice but we ended up with a late night and a late start (I mean we're both late now and heading out the door), so just to remind you you're coming round at eightish tomorrow…no ifs or ands or buts. Bring Julia if she gets back."

"Sure, thanks…I'll be there, with or without."

I made a second huge mug of tea, working up to a shower and another hectic schedule of doing nothing. Life goes on, I thought, normality for Julia, for Ray and Sian, whilst I re-assessed what had last night seemed like my own private hell, and seemed only slightly less so this morning. I found myself dissecting what Julia had said, suddenly sifting it for any hint of a lie, aware how ridiculously paranoid this was, as well as how ironic and what a sorry pass I was coming too; but Julia was a very attractive woman…a somewhat neglected attractive woman far away from home…so why not? Conflicting voices, my conflicting voices, one attributing my own subversive logic to Julia, argued the toss.

Then there was Sian, calm and collected, breakfasted and no doubt immaculate, ready to kiss Ray goodbye as they parted to begin their lucrative working day…late. What had been their late night, not the restaurant, that's for sure. Lurid images of the two of them, tipsy, tumbling out of the taxi and fucking on the stairs. I just about made it to the toilet and vomited the tea and then the alcoholic bile, then nothing, but retching still. The shower brought little relief.

Chapter 19

What a difference there can be between the inner and outer life; between the personal and the public self. I wonder now if it is perhaps the case that a wide dissonance between these two, so wide that they became irreconcilable, might be a major factor in the "breakdown," or, to be more accurate, the onset of mental illness; a variation on the idea of the "Split personality." I was acutely aware of my fragility then. How could I not be?

Of course in my particular situation I was well aware of which was the "real me," so to speak, but bound to supress it, to act out a part which denied the horrendous inner conflicts I was suffering, and to hide the doubts that lurked, vague and sinister shapes within me. They swirled, solidifying and dispersing like a swamp mist. Were they based on anything real, or were they spawned by my own over active imagination, the result of morbid rumination and analysis? What was real…I didn't know.

This was bad enough, without even beginning to consider my own duplicity and guilt. These had seemed to be much easier to deal with at the start, but were not so now. Before, I really had felt like a Master of the Universe, pursuing a noble cause, my own personal Holy Grail, against which nothing could stand. My hapless victim (Julia) was OK in the short term, and in the longer would be assisted to a "soft landing." The other potential casualty (Ray) was my friend, but had his own conscience to reconcile so did not weigh too much on mine. Minor considerations of morality and personal integrity were swept aside by my unshakable belief in my love for Sian, and hers for me. The end was already writ, and it was our duty to do anything that had to be done in order to bring it about.

It was not so simple now, as doubt crept about like the half heard scuttling of a mouse in the night. The grand deception was not as grand as it had seemed, as truth and beauty became themselves objects of suspicion. Furtive disguise was now the order of the day, with not even the woman I loved, the woman at the centre of my being, privy to my innermost thoughts, secretive and hid.

Ray was a good friend to me and this was becoming harder to deal with. Julia, the hapless victim seemed less hapless, less like a victim now, the mantle passing imperceptibly to me. I was like a Japanese guerrilla fighter isolated in a jungle far from home, not knowing if the emperor's great cause was still alive but fighting still, surviving on the love and duty stored in the battery of his heart, fearing oblivion, no such thing as honourable defeat.

An hour had passed, perhaps two, sitting in an armchair haunted by a confusion of thoughts and feelings. Frightened, but like the Japanese soldier, or the gambler past the point of no return, only able to go on, unable to turn around and retrace my steps. Showered and shaved, there I sat, immobilised, vaguely thinking that I ought to eat something.

The phone rang. It was Sian, not the "Ray and Sian" Sian, but my lover, tender and intimate. You know what they say about the heart leaping, well it's true, it can, mine did. She caressed the phone with her voice:

"Oh Callum, my darling, my love, you sounded so awful earlier, and I just had to pretend. Tell me it's not me my love, I'm so frightened, I need you, I want you."

The words tumbled out and my ghosts vanished, cast out of me in a split second. All was well.

"No darling, it's not you, it's nothing, I just miss you so, not seeing you this week, sometimes it gets me down…" she interrupted me:

"Callum, I've had a cancellation, can we meet, soon…now? I'm…oh god I'm getting wet…I so want you."

"Oh Sian yes, just come round my darling, just come here."

"But are you sure, what if someone sees…Julia…"

She came and we made love in my bed, in Julia's and my bed. Wordless I let her in and we climbed the stairs to the bedroom. We stood, kissing, long and deep, tenderly yet trembling both, hands gently undoing each other's clothes. Her green silk dress slid noiselessly down her stockings to the floor, the merest frosting of fine white lace between her legs, a taut transparent tracery cupping her breasts. As I kicked off my jeans she reached behind her back, and spilled her tits from her bra, looking at me watching her, inviting as she held it out to the side and let it drop.

I tentatively reached out and lightly touched the side of her breast, but made no move, drinking her in as with her hands sweeping her hair back and up, she paused, posing wantonly for a second or two, revelling in my gaze moving over her, but panting, I could see. I grabbed the nipple now and roughly pulled her squealing up against me, mouths colliding, consuming one another like half-starved things; she grabbed my cock and dragged me down onto the bed, less composed now, pulling me roughly onto her, legs spread wide, frantic, gasping:

"Get it in! For Christ's sake get it in me…fuck me…just FUCK ME!"

 I yanked aside her pants at her bidding to push up into her hot wet cunt, knowing without an atom of doubt that this was my final surrender…it would always be this way…it was complete. I wanted to be vanquished… was already.

Chapter 20

I decided to cry off the dinner invitation, telling Sian I felt it may be awkward with Ray, and sensing she was relieved as she readily agreed. My real reason was quite different. I needed to protect this small capsule of peace, to seal it against the world. I did not want to witness Sian and Ray's "domestic bliss," their casual affection for one another, to see them together in their home. I feared the return of doubts, of suspicions, of uncertainty. I was not able to see the slight flaw in this "ostrich" logic. I was committed. I *had* to believe.

Looking for distraction, Saturday saw me making an early start and driving down to Derbyshire to walk up Kinder Scout. It was a cold steel grey December day, the wind sharp and carrying stop-start flurries of snow. I had too much time alone doing nothing, too easy to think, and I did not want to think. What was it Sian had whispered to me not long since, her finger pressed against my lips... "Let us just be, my love, it will come, all will be well." I clung to these words and thought I saw a deeper wisdom there. All would be well. I saw a white hare sprinting down a snow flecked run of scree, and walked for miles, revelling in the physical exertion. The icy wind and the imperturbable vastness of the terrain had the calming effect of making my petty worries and concerns seem insubstantial, dwarfed in the larger perspective of all this. Our love was part of this, immutable, just there, and all we had to do was to be.

I found a tiny crowded pub in Hayfield, a few walkers mingling with a friendly local crowd, home-made steak and kidney pie and Theakstons ales, a cavernous inglenook heaped with logs, Christmas decorations sagging around the bar. I felt mellow and warmed. Life was not so complicated. Here I was in the real world with real people enjoying themselves on Saturday afternoon. My neurotic ruminations seemed preposterous now. Sian loved me. She was probably waiting for me to take control of the situation and move things along, instead of which I dithered and doubted and tied myself in knots, immobilised by my own ridiculous imaginings. Sian loved me. I could see it. It was plain to see, and how often had she told me. All would be well.

As I drove home the light was fading and the moors merging with December's early dusk. I thought that we might buy a place here, in Hayfield or perhaps in Glossop, Sian and I. Sian worked from home and travelled widely anyway, and I...well perhaps the fantasy of our own business was not so ridiculous, but in any case, something would come up. The detail didn't matter.

Chapter 21

We were soon well into the Christmas round of drinks and parties. Julia was making friends and influencing people at work, and I was dragged along to one or two dos as not quite the trophy husband. I didn't mind so much, and in some ways it was quite good to reconnect with some of my old colleagues from work, and to escape the local scene, where I felt increasingly edgy. Julia was obviously well thought of and popular as ever at work, though the flip side of this was that I was even more acutely aware of my own inertia.

The fact was that I had not been seriously looking for employment for some time, and when Julia suggested I look at jobs that were advertised I always found reasons why they would not suit. I'd realized that with a nine -to -five job, my already insufficient time with Sian would be impossibly small. Once we lived together it would be different, but for now I had decided to tread water, much to Julia's frustration.

I stopped going to five a side as I didn't want to get into further conversations with Ray, and let it be known that I had a lingering ankle problem. Generally I found myself where possible tending to avoid socializing. My previously cocky and blasé attitude to seeing Sian and Ray at social events had given way to an indefinable nervousness and apprehension. This was nothing to do with worries about being found out, and everything to do with not wanting to see the two of them together ,or to have to listen to Ray's laddish banter. I had to control my world which felt much more fragile than it had been before. I was the antelope at the watering hole drinking carefully, eyes casting nervously about, muscles tense and twitching, ready to leap aside, no longer confident or at ease in the anonymity of the herd.

All of this had its effect on me and inevitably on Julia too. I haunted the flat like the ghost of Christmas past. My sure fire wit and repartee was less sure and infrequently fired. Julia became irritated with me and increasingly did her own thing. I slept late and increasingly badly. I failed miserably in my attempts to resurrect my meditation practice from bygone years. In Buddhist meditation you are required to focus on the breathing, and as the expected procession of uninvited thoughts comes up, to briefly examine each thought and let it go, returning each time to the breath. Rather than having the desired calming effect, examining my thoughts led each time to a state of high anxiety, and I gave up.

It was a life of avoidance, and I knew full well that this was the case. I was confronting nothing, resigned to being a passive prisoner of the situation I had created. I was avoiding confronting my own doubts, or anything which might in some way validate them; but knowing the malaise does not mean knowing the cure. I doubted everything. I doubted myself. I was paralysed.

I knew of course that this situation couldn't be sustained for long, but far from moving me to action, it caused me to cling desperately to what I had. I told myself that in the New Year I was going to be more assertive with Sian about moving our relationship on to a proper footing and ending the deception. I would tell her that waiting for Ray to decide to move in with his dancer was obviously a "wing and a prayer," that I was not prepared to sit it out any longer. She evidently feared the trauma and upheaval that forcing the issue would bring, which is why she avoided the subject. I would support her, I would speak to Ray. I would do it in the New Year once Christmas was done and dusted.

In the meantime Sian and I usually managed to meet a couple of times a twice a week, more if she could get away. She *was* insatiable. This was a comfort (as well as a joy). Her voice on the phone drew me like a rising cobra to the snake charmers tune. She promised everything, and delivered every time with interest. Such sex. It eclipsed everything else. Welcome to the pleasure dome.

Thinking back to what I said before about most "love" affairs being essentially "sex" affairs, it would be disingenuous to protest that ours was the exception. This is the mould into which clandestine assignations are inevitably compressed. The mechanics and constraints of the "affair" strip it down to essentials. Precious moments. Constraints of time and place and danger conspire to reduce, to synthesise love into an extreme abandonment to lust, protesting the desperate and difficult circumstances of lives spent apart. Here there is catharsis, tempering the on-going distress. Wild aberration or the purest refinement? Perhaps both.

But in any case there is one thing that *is* true: whatever the obstacles which prevent you from being together and loving one another as you would wish to, being able to fuck each other senseless from time to time really helps.

Chapter 22

"So do you still fancy Cordoba?" A wet Sunday in early February, and Julia and I were indulging our usual routine with the papers in bed; she had the Travel Guide.

"Yeah," I murmured without lifting my head from the Review, "...sounds good to me." Well I could hardly say otherwise really, and in any case it did. The thought of those ancient Moorish streets basking in the hot Andalucian sunshine was nothing if not appealing in our dismal Mancunian winter.

"Oh, don't kill me with enthusiasm. I seem to remember you were quite keen on the idea when we were broke. What was it, some sort of flower festival or something around my birthday?"

I capitulated: "Patio festival. Yeah, it's in May, I remember. All the locals open up their patios so you can wander round them, and for a small consideration you can have your pick of the women, unless of course you've been daft enough to bring one."

"Ha bloody ha; and anyway who'd be bringing who...I mean, I might *just* consider taking you (read: "paying for you") if you're *very, very* good."

I sighed deeply and dropped my head, "You really know how to hurt Jules, there was no need for that."

She put down the paper and snuggled in "Oh darling I'm sorreeee, I was only winding you up..."

"Hah! Don't mess vith zee master...!" and my tickling fingers were all over her, her screams winning no respite until she begged for mercy.

"Bastard!" she said, but jumped half out of bed as I feigned a renewed assault; then in the whiniest voice imaginable, "Ohhhhh be nice to me darling..." and snuggling in properly now she slid her hand down my belly. Oh; her fingers had closed around my balls; not squeezing tight but with a very firm grip that would not be easily dislodged.

Sensible maternal voice: "Have you got something to say darling?" her fingers tightened just a little, hardly perceptibly...but perceptibly.

"Oh come on Jules..."

"Just one teensy weensy little word ....you know I hate being tickled my darling...and you know you regret it, so let's just hear that one little word, Mmmmmmm?"

Very quietly: "Sorry."

"Pardon darling, I didn't quite catch that. Did you say something to me?"

Cough; pause: "Sorry Julia."

Hand relaxing turning, collecting my cock, squeezing and gently pulling as she continued: "There, good boy, and don't you feel better for saying that....ooooh you *do*!"

Christmas and New Year had come and gone. I was more reclusive than ever, except for seeing Sian, and I had been joined in hibernation by Julia. She was working hard and all hours, with little energy left for socializing, and anyway there was the post festive lull. I had earned brownie points for applying for a couple of jobs she'd spotted. I'd made every effort with the application forms (assisted of course by Julia), but deliberately flunked the interviews. I was careful to be suitably disappointed when I received knock backs for both, especially the second one. Having learned the potential benefits from the first run out, I had enthused about it and given Julia to believe that I was quietly hopeful.

There were significant rewards for this. Julia saw how hard I'd apparently tried. To some extent she felt that she was responsible, having cajoled me into it, for my disappointment and my generally quite low mood which she attributed to me not being able to be a useful person. She was solicitous and kind, and when I suggested applying for another post for which I knew I could very obviously not be in the running, (and of course she knew this too), I allowed her to gently dissuade me.

We knew each other so well, and in spite of all it was actually very easy for Julia and I to hibernate together. Julia was kind and supportive, having formed the view that I might be depressed, and rallying to help me through. She was unwittingly glad when I went out on whatever pretext to meet Sian, wanting me to go out more and be happy. She kept me sane, without ever knowing what cargo was aboard this drifting hulk that she had in tow.

"So what about it then?" We were nestled together post coital, her head on my chest.

"What…again…already…you really are insatiable!"

"Stupid." She humphed, drawing in closer, slinging a leg over and nuzzling up into my neck. "We could both do with getting away and some sunshine. Cordoba in May *would* be lovely."

I felt momentarily safe; Julia's familiar body wrapping me up, her spiky blond hair low in my peripheral vision, her voice, trusting, caring offering to take me away from all this.

"Would you like to Jules? I mean, seriously, it's your dosh. Maybe we should wait till I find something. I mean it's *your* bloody birthday we're talking about. I really hate this."

"My treat," she whispered, and that was that, as with a little squeeze she snoozed off. So, we were going to Cordoba after all.

Chapter 23

Why did I continue with it? Was it worth it? Julia was a star. The detrimental effects on my life in the short term were plainly visible, and in the long term potentially catastrophic. Surely at some point sense would prevail, and the "fling" would be sacrificed for the greater good. If only it had been that simple.

Yes, I was like a blind man fumbling along from one assignation to the next, but each one was a revelation. There was no abatement in the excitement, quite the contrary, the promise was always exceeded, the bar continually raised. The planned rendezvous were navigational beacons which dominated my vision, and the breathless phone calls for a spontaneous meeting were looked for, craved, the source of such a rush of pleasure that I cannot begin to describe.

We were seared by a flame… I will call it love, as nothing else will do. There was a distillation of sexual desire, abandon, all inhibition and restraint was shed. I had total freedom with Sian's body and she with mine. To ask was to receive, the more "off limits," the better, and although we both were very adventurous, there was never a refusal. Her pleasure was mine, mine hers, a twister of joy. Sometimes we were symbiotically intimate gentle, deeply absorbed in each other. At others we would rut like animals, taking, shagging as if the others body was there for this purpose alone. Sian was an exhibitionist; she loved to strip and perform sexually for me; it was her thing.

It would be an unhurried, tantalising affair. She would have me sit on a chair, beginning with a coy strip and dance, then more sexually explicit stuff. She had no boundaries and sometimes would bring herself off as I watched…needing me to watch. I was not allowed to move and she would allow me fondle and lick her, fleeting tasters at first then more prolonged as she undressed me , to wait upon her pleasure, climbing on and off my cock like a No 9 bus…and much, much more.

I still see one image of Sian, naked but for her heels, like a ballerina frozen in a grand plié but impaled on the fingers of my extended hand, legs splayed out and bent at right angles, hands resting on knees and eyes closed, pushing right down onto my knuckles, where for an eternity she did not move at all, her breath coming in short staccato gasps as I felt her tremble like a small bird stuck on lime.

When finally we fucked, on the chair, bed, floor against the wall… wherever, we would be mad for each other. There was a fusion, a coming home at last, gripping tight and shagging, no escape , no quarter given, fierce kisses…so many kisses… and all the adoring dirty talk that whipped along the dogs of our desire.

At last we'd collapse replete in each other's arms; gentle kisses now and murmurings of love. There would be quiet tears which I did not understand, but held her shivering in my arms.

We revelled in each other, in the excess. We talked about hiring a prostitute for a threesome though we never actually did. It was Sian's idea. She wanted to watch me shagging another woman… to join in and for them both to take me in turns and together. She would have sex with the woman too…would I like that…?

This was Sian.

So the sensible attraction of warmth and domesticity with Julia, even with good sex and great friendship did not compete with this fire. The nature of fire, of course, is that it burns as well as illuminates; and it did burn, it consumed my life beyond the flame, sucked it in as fuel for my endless desire; but the flame itself grew ever brighter, the fabled "blinding light."

Endless desire; well that is the nature of desire. It can be sated but never requited…freedom that imprisons, consummation that consumes. Perhaps it is only within the constrained and rarefied atmosphere of the clandestine "affair" that desire can thrive with such intensity for so long, and with such disregard to all else; and perhaps this is the greatest love, the essence of a love which cannot fully flower, channelled into this narrow and turbulent torrent of secret sex with the unattainable partner. Who can say not?... it is a heady cocktail, a powerful drug.

Chapter 24

It was Friday night, and Julia was late home from work. I had been with Sian in the afternoon, showered and changed, and was out of the doldrums that weighed on me day to day. We had had a gentle time after Monday's fireworks, loving and tender. Unusually we had only fucked once. Even though out of work I was in weekend mode, anticipating a meal out with Julia, and yes, fucking her too. I couldn't help it, having Julia on the same day as Sian turned me on…and my excitement turned Julia on too, so what the hell, everyone was happy.

I heard the car and opened the front door, Jules handing me her briefcase en passant, flopping into the armchair. She kicked off her shoes and ordering a la Father Ted "Drink!"

"Coming up," I said, heading for the tonic from fridge.

"Err, actually, I think I'll have a glass of wine."

"Really? Ok. Where've you been anyway?"

"Oh, didn't I say? I had a doctor's appointment and just went straight there."

"No, you didn't; why, what's the matter?" I handed her the wine and settled back with my G&T. "Good day?"

Sprawled like a rag doll, eyes closed, Jules grunted something that might have been yes or no.

I really felt as if I'd been at work and had earned my gin and some R&R too. We nursed our drinks, and I got up to put on some music…something for me to wind down to…

"What do you fancy?"

She opened her eyes and smiled, a tired lovely smile.

"No, don't put anything on darling, not just yet...come here," and she dangled a floppy hand in the air for me to take, which I obediently did, kneeling on the floor and sliding my other hand up her skirt.

"*Stop it...**Callum**...*just...can we have a bit of calm please...just....there! *Good* boy!" She patronized as I settled back and she adjusted her dress.

"You've got that look Jules."

"Have I?"

"You know you have! Alright, spill. What have you done? What have you bought? Ah...you've been promoted and you're the new CEO..."

"Callum, I'm pregnant."

My heart was pounding in my ears and momentarily I blurred, seeing Julia's smile fall from her face, hearing myself as from a distance.

"Julia?...but you can't...I mean...it's not possible...is it?...oh god, Julia, it's...bloody hell...it's...amazing!"

Julia had taken both my hands. She was leaning forward and had brought my hands into her lap her face close to mine, repeating my name. "Callum, **Callum**...*Callum*! are you alright? You've gone white!"

I tried to compose myself, to smile, to say something coherent, something *happy*!

"Oh I'm sorry Jules, it must be shock. Are you sure? It's...well, it's amazing..."

Julia was looking at me querulously now.

"Is that amazing biologically speaking, or amazing wonderful? Callum, are you not happy?"

I could see that she was going to cry, and gathering myself pulled her to me and hugged her tight.

"Oh my darling, of course I'm happy, of course it's wonderful, you clever, clever girl!" I held her tight and wouldn't let her go, afraid my face might give me away.

She was crying; no, she was laughing…both and she forced herself free, and kissed me.

"Callum, darling, we've done it; we're going to have a baby! The doctor's sure. She can't explain it, says it's a one in a million chance but it happens sometimes. Oh Callum!" And now she *was* crying, arms around my neck, tears flowing freely soaking into my T shirt as I rubbed her back and shushed her.

"Hey, come on, I'm here, shhhhhhh; clever you. She'll be like you. She'll be clever to." I was talking nonsense, saying the first things to come into my head, and now Julia was laughing again, raining kisses on my face.

"You sweet, sweet man! Anyway, how do you know it's going to be a girl?" and eyes agog in shock horror… "What if it's twins…!?"

I smiled now and held her hand. How could I not be happy for her? And I was, truly happy for her, though even then there was a knot inside. This was the end for Sian and me, even I could see that. This one could not be swept aside with all the rest.

"Come on!" she said, jumping to her feet and hauling me up too. "We're getting changed and going out…hey, why don't you ring Ray and Sian and make a night of it?"

"No…*god* no…just us Jules, anyway we shouldn't be telling people yet darling. You know… the first few weeks and all that?"

"Yes, you're right…on both counts. This is *our* night, and we'd best not broadcast it yet. How thoughtful you can be!" She gave me a big hug and dashed off upstairs.

I slumped down again into the chair with a sigh, relieved for that quick thinking at least…I would have a few weeks more of Sian before she knew, before I had to give her up. And who could say…the first few weeks *are* risky after all, even *I* knew that, and with Julia's age and complications…not that I would have wished… oh Christ…I poured another drink.

Chapter 25

What was for Julia the fulfilment of a suppressed dream, a flowering, a joyful opening up of her life, to me signified an ending, the loss of the thing I held most precious. I was obliged to smile and feign…something…god knows…imbecilic joy… as I counted down the few remaining days of love. The weekend seemed endless, and I prayed for Monday when I could be spared the pretence of the happy father to be and doting partner, when I could see my lover, fuck her, and fuck her.

Fortunately I was able to drown my sorrows on the Friday and Saturday night, rather over celebrating the joyous tidings but excused my excesses. The resulting hangovers came in handy too, festering in bed with a sore head excused me temporarily from pre fatherly duties.

Julia was so happy, fortunately to the point of distraction, in her own little maternal world, one she had never thought to see. I had not appreciated before just how keenly felt her apparent inability to conceive must have been beneath the many philosophical layers of fatalism where she had hidden it away. Then again, she was always a glass half full person, and we had a nice easy life to be sure. I'd thought it was more of a problem for *me,* all those years ago when we had been told. I could, after all, father a child and would have wanted to then. What an irony that this unforeseen but once desired pregnancy should be welcomed as the ruination of all my hopes and dreams.

I wondered too whether there may have been a tiny element of Julia seeing this unforeseen development as a fillip to our relationship. It is something that you hear about, a commonplace occurrence: couples looking to add meaning to their lives and direction to their ailing relationships. The perfect scapegoat perhaps… but one which, having loaded your troubles onto it, you have to keep.

I adopted the 'sensible' approach, building on my initial success about no premature announcements, and deterring Julia from any level of detailed talk or billing and cooing about gender, names, planning a nursery and so forth. We were not to tempt fate or to explicitly make plans until Julia was over the high risk period of the early weeks.

The fact that I took a certain amount of comfort and practical relief from this as it were 'window' of high risk to the well-being of my partner and unborn child was plainly abhorrent, despicable, and I duly despised myself for it; but that is how it was. My love for Sian, my desire, already overwhelming, obsessional, was ratcheted up to a level of febrile urgency in the lengthening shadow of its impending loss. I was in every sense, beyond the pale.

Monday came and at last Sian picked me up. We'd decided to go for a drive and have sex in the car or outside if it was warm enough. "You're just a tart," Id commented.

"Oh, I can do tart Callum….would you like me to?" had been the velveteen riposte.

Oh and she could! Fresh from Primark, white shiny stilettos, bare legs and pink lycra mini skirt complete with gold chain belt. Best of all though, her bra less tits bursting through a virtually transparent white lycra top. She was chewing gum.

"De ye like it?" she said in broad Mancunian. *She* obviously liked it, her nipples hugely erect and I palmed and tweaked them as we kissed.

"Hang on chuck, don't…" she pushed my hand away, "Wait till we're down 't road!"

We were in luck. It was an unseasonably warm sunny day. I slid my hand up her skirt as she drove.

"Cheeky!" she scolded, immediately opening her legs. No knickers of course and her cunt running like a tap. I frigged her all the way, to the delight of the truck drivers, Sian chewing more and more rapidly, panting and moaning, jerking her hips and periodically telling me with one or two minor variations that it was "Fuckin' great."

By the time we turned along a forestry track off a quiet B-road Sian was soaked and frantic. The car was hardly stopped and she was out and leaning over the boot, yanking her skirt up around her waist, legs spread wide.

"Go on then ye bastard, shag me…just shag me!" She shouted. I was behind her, her cunt pink and wet, her cheeks and thighs shone wet with cunt juice too. What a time for my zip to get stuck. "For fucks sake Callum, get it in me!" She was wiggling her bum impatiently, and glanced impatiently behind as I pulled out my cock, hugely erect. She widened her stance and quickly reached back, pulling her cheeks wide apart; *everything* was wet… "Take yer pick luv… "

We found a small pub and had a drink and a snack in a quiet alcove. It was virtually deserted apart from a couple of lads playing pool in the public bar. Sian had a cheese roll but I wasn't hungry and made do with the beer. She'd reverted to posh Cheshire for lunch, shades of the "Absolutely Fabulous" Joanna Lumley character…and despite having stuck her chewing gum on the side of her glass.

"Mmmmmm I'm starving," she said, "*Really* nice cheese," and ate with relish at the same time as casually taking my hand, opening her legs and pushing it up her skirt. I cast a nervous glance over the edge of the cubicle toward the bar where the ancient landlord was reading the paper, and I obediently frigged her as she ate.

I watched her with interest, turned on but fascinated too.

"What's the beer like" she said, quite normally, though tilting her hips in time with my fingers.

"Not bad," I said, "Pretty good actually."

She took another bite of her roll "This is lovely" she said, "*Really* nice…" but I pushed right up and she gasped, "…*really* nice cheese," she gasped again on an intake of breath, putting the roll down now and covering her mouth with her hand to stop the noise of her panting.

"Mmm, you already said that darling," I said, smiling. I glanced again over to the bar. No change there…and I nodded reassuringly to Sian, turning toward her and resting my arm on the back of the cubicle. I could see the bar whilst getting in deeper, feeling her growing urgency as she pushed her hot sopping cunt onto my fingers, eyes bulging, her hand still clamped on her mouth.

She came with a loud cry and I was immediately on my feet, pulling her up as the landlord started and called across alarmed, "Everything alright?"

"Yes... yes thanks!" I said, grabbing her bag as I ushered her toward the door, tottering on her heels, skirt indecent and silly grin at Mein Host, all but a neon sign on her head reading 'Bimbo.'

"My wife's just a little unwell, some fresh air should do the trick..." as I noticed the large wet patch on the back of her skirt and with a strangled cry clamped her bag against it, forcing a smile of camaraderie at the goggle eyed landlord. "Forget her head if it wasn't screwed on...!"

We fell out the door in hysterics, still giggling uncontrollably in the car. It was a minute before we could speak. Sian recovered first:

"Where now?" she said.

"I think... back to the forestry."

"...'a was 'oping ye'd say that chuck," she whispered, and she was backing the car round. I lifted her top so her tits tumbled into view cupping one, satisfyingly heavy in my hand, as Sian with a smile waved regally and blew a kiss to the landlord as we passed him on the pub steps, newspaper in hand , jaw sagged open .

Chapter 26

When Sian dropped me off near home I watched the car disappear, blowing a kiss and standing undecided what to do. Now she was gone, and everything closed in again, worse than before. How could I be without her? I wandered up Lapwing Lane to the shops, then drifted along to the Dave's for some company and distraction.

Dave let me in with a squeal of delight.

"Callum! Where've *you* been stranger? Come in. What's the matter… lost a pound and found a penny? Mmm, no, there's something else….Callum's post coital, isn't Callum?"

I was dumbstruck. The man had sixth sense! He was looking at me, one eyebrow raised.

Mmmmmm?"

"Knock it off Dave." I slumped on the couch.

"Well what's that on your flies then?" I hurriedly glanced down.

"Oooooooooooh, guilty as charged! You naughty boy!"

"Knock it *off* Dave! Anyway Julia's at work."

"And…?" he drummed his fingers on the arm of the chair.

I looked away, despite myself a huge sigh escaping, and my head sinking.

"Oh fuck…FUCK…FUCK!"

Dave was sat next to me in an instant, his hand on my arm…

"Oh Callum. Oh look I'm sorry. I was only… "

I couldn't look at him.

"Is this an affair of the dick, or an affair of the heart?" he said kindly.

I leaned forward, burying my face in my hands, "Oh fucking hell Dave, I don't know what to do!"

"The heart… oh bloody hell Callum." We sat quietly for a minute, Dave stroking my arm. He gave it a squeeze.

"I'm going to make a nice cup of tea, then we'll have a talk."

I stared out of the window, and absently watched the trees catching the sun, ruffled in a light breeze. There was a sense of relief, but already I knew I couldn't tell him all, and here I was, bringing my shadowy half-truth world to my friend.

Dave poured the tea.

"Look, I don't want you to tell me who she is. Just tell me Callum, do you love her?"

I slumped back in the chair.

"Yeah I do. I do. It's…it's…" I couldn't finish the sentence, and Dave interjected.

"Just take your time, slow down. What about Julia?"

"I love Julia too, she's my pal…more than that, but…it's not the same. I'm finished Dave…I don't know what to do. Whatever I do it'll be wrong!"

"Does Julia know?"

"God no…she'd leave."

"How would you feel if she did, that's the million dollar question Callum?"

I stood up; it was getting out of hand.

"I dunno… I **don't** know! It can't happen…you don't understand! Oh fucking hell Dave, it's a mess! I shouldn't have dragged you into it."

"*Whoa*…hey…just sit down. And tough titty you've told me now so that's that; but you haven't dragged me into it Callum. I'm not *in* it at all, so just stop that nonsense. I'm here for you, I'm your mate, that's all there is to it."

I sat down. My hands were trembling and my eyes prickling.

Dave kept his counsel and I breathed, trying to regain some control, slowly feeling the tears recede.

"Sorry… sorry. And thanks. I can't…I need to think."

"Yeah. Sure. You do. Leave it now if you like. But I'm here. Listen? I'm here. Come and talk about it any time darling." He slipped an arm round me and gave me a little cuddle.

"Christ Dave don't do that, you'll have me blubbing!"

"Yes, well, that might not be such a bad thing. Drink your tea before it gets cold."

We sat, sipping our tea, it was tepid already in the tiny china cups, and we put our cups and saucers down together. I was making as to go, and Dave put his hand on my arm and stayed me.

"Callum I haven't got any answers, but I love Julia, and I love you, and I'll just say this. The fireworks go, don't they, with the years? The voltage goes down, and it will with this other one too. You need to decide if there's still current enough to light your fairy lights…you know…the ones at home. Hey, that's quite poetic isn't it?" He smiled, and I had to too.

"Thanks…really…thanks…"

"Whenever you want, our kid… I'm right *here*."

I trailed off home. I hadn't of course told him about Julia; conveniently left out that minor detail. He'd find out soon enough, and what would he think of me then? That's when they come unstuck, the promises people make to be even handed and remain friends with both the breaking up couple… when they find out that one of them's an out and out bastard. I shouldn't have told him; no matter, I had, and I was glad I had.

Chapter 27

Julia was so happy. It was impossible not to be happy for her. Whilst I couldn't quite march alongside her, I was doing my best not to rain on her parade. She wanted to talk about the baby, about all aspects of the future. My feeble attempts to hold back this tidal wave of enthusiasm were in vain.

It all became very real when I went with her to the doctor, and she talked about an early scan and later, the likelihood of hospitalisation for most of the final trimester. Julia was seven weeks gone, and the doctor was reassuring, saying that there was not a hugely greater likelihood of miscarriage for Julia from this point than for any other woman. The delivery itself might be more problematic and possibly require a planned caesarean, but the message was a confident one: this baby was going to happen; a miracle conception followed by a well- planned professionally managed pregnancy and birth.

We walked home hand in hand. I'd given in, it was real and it was going to happen. Stop fighting it Callum, a voice inside me said, and I felt something loosen if not let go. We were both quiet. Julia snuggled in and I put my arm around her, kissing her hair. She was not who I wanted her to be, but I knew that I loved her in spite of all I had done to her… was still doing to her. What was it I'd said to Dave… "She's my pal…more than that." Well it was true enough…quite a lot more.

We walked along home and set about food. More wine for me nowadays as Julia had given up the booze, and after dinner I nursed a third glass, with Julia snuggled up to me on the couch. It was like having your own pet koala.

"Callum."

"Mmm?"

"Are you happy?"

"Mmm."

She paused. There was more to come. I felt it. Not just a question of discussing practicalities as we two became three in our modest flat and me unemployed, but, how can I describe it, bonding stuff, talking about our baby, about us, about…our baby, there, inside Julia. I knew she had to, *we* had to. In a way, there at that moment I wanted to, wanted to be close to her, to fall into this safe haven, to share my lonely barren life with this lovely woman. How I wanted this to be the case. If I tried, if I really tried, could I not return her love in equal measure, find goodness and truth once again?

I put down my glass and held her. "What's on your mind Jules?"

She turned her smiling face up to mine.

"Hmmm?"

She was like a large contented cat, except I knew better. "Out with it smiler, tell Callum what devilry you're brewing up, and he may decide not to beat you."

"You can't beat me," she bleated, "I'm pregnant, AND I've got contact lenses!" She snuggled in again

"Brute."(Pause). "Callum…"

"Yes Julia?"

"Do you love me?"

"Yes Julia."

"And the baby?"

"No Julia, I haven't met him yet."

"It could be a she, and anyway, you should love it, it's your baby too."

"That's what *you* say. I'm not answering any further questions till my lawyer's present, and I claim protection under the 5th amendment."

"Wrong country fellah, you're stuffed"

"No, your stuffed…allegedly…wanna try it again?" as I ran my hand up her skirt.

"Hah!" hand retrieved and victoriously slapped, "You said AGAIN…so you admit it was you the first time…game set and match…take me to the church."

"OK so I'm an easy lay" hand sliding up skirt again in between legs, "But I only have a mental age of 13…technically it's under age rape," fingers making good progress into pants."

"Callum!" excessive emphasis on the "lum," followed by small fists raining blows on me as I retreat to the other end of the couch, where I skulk, smelling my fingers for consolation.

"You really are disgusting."

"Who loves ya baby."

Softening, "Alright, darling, you can love me lots… when we've had a talk."

"But I'm only 13…OK….OK let's talk."

Julia was sitting up straight now, and I knew immediately that this might not be something I wanted to hear.

"Darling I need to tell my Mum. I want us to go down and see them on Sunday."

I considered the options. This was not so much a request as a statement of what was going to happen. Julia was close to her mother;

less so her father who I couldn't stand and which was reciprocated. There was nothing to be gained by arguing.

"OK." I said, quietly.

"Will you come?" Julia had obviously been expecting s a tussle and was tentative, still waiting for some kind of protest or resistance.

"Sure, of course. I'm not going to let you take all the credit."

She edged over and took my hand. "Thanks." We kissed, soft and tender, and amid the confusion of feelings I was turned on, and not just me. I felt my hand taken, guided up her skirt again and placed firmly between her legs, hers sliding over to ease down my zip.

"Now you can love me lots…and lots."

Chapter 28

That was on the Tuesday. I slept badly, beset by misgivings that reared up in the night as Julia slept, returning again with a redoubled cold insistence not to be denied in the wee hours. I wanted to wake Julia and tell her it was a mistake, it wasn't too late, she could get an abortion.

Wednesday morning saw the sun blazing brightly as if mocking me and my morbid ruminations. Julia was in fine fettle, and my spirits rose a little too, buoyed by her exuberance and sheer joie de vivre; buoyed also by the prospect of a precious day with Sian…much more precious now, and I was not going to squander our remaining hours together.

We met around ten thirty. Sian was early, and I spotted the car in the appointed layby, gleaming in the dappled sunlight filtering through the trees. Unusually Sian got out of the car to greet me as I approached, and not for the first time I had to do a double take….was this woman really my lover…disbelief as she embraced and kissed me, drowning in her lips, her perfume; my pulse quickened pounding in my ears. She was as elegant as I'd ever seen her. A fine cashmere sweater, pastel green; a simple white cotton pencil skirt, split with skin tone silk stockings…hold ups judging from the smooth contours of her thighs; beige leather shoes, heels of course… expensive. She had her hair up, with small gold stud earrings and an intricately worked gold chain, eastern perhaps. We drove up to Saddleworth and booked into a B&B in Delph

Delph is one of the Saddleworth villages, built from hard grey millstone grit, and tucked away in wrinkles on the edge of the moor. A mill village, like all the rest… Denshaw, Dobcross, Uppermill, Diggle and Greenfield. They were colonized by the Manchester well to do from the 1960s on, with property prices rocketing as the flight to rural commuter land gathered pace, tourism burgeoning alongside.

The B&B was an old terrace on the narrow main street, with small stone mullioned windows which I remember being told were to avoid high window taxes rather than for any practical or aesthetic reason. There were the statutory low beamed ceilings and creaky old wooden floorboards, and a staid spinster owner, twin set and pearls, whose instant disapproval was evident: "Oh. Do you have any luggage to bring in?"

Sian caught the drift, and replied in her best cut glass, "No darling just our bodies, that's all we'll be needing…could we have a look at the room?"

The lady was unphased but steely polite as she showed us into a slightly cluttered room with old rather than antique furnishings, including a high sprung bed with an attractive inlaid mahogany headboard, and fortunately a modern mattress.

"This will be fine," Sian said, "Thank you ever so much, Mr Smith and I are going to have a little… erm… afternoon nap now," smiling sweetly as the lady forced a tight twitch of a polite smile.

"Yes…well…enjoy your stay," and she hurried away closing the door.

"You really shouldn't you know," I gathered her in and she kissed me.

"Callum. God I've missed you." We could hear cars passing and people talking in the street, but as we kissed and held each other we were in a bubble, always the same, flowing in and out of one another in a temporary time warp while the world went on around us.

Sian kicked off her shoes and with no more ado undressed and lay on the bed, naked but for the gold necklace. She was smiling, lying on her side, her head propped on her hand, waiting for me. I looked at her as I often did, and she lay motionless happy for me to look. Her large full breasts in this position lolled lazily heavy, ripe and alluring. At first she watched me looking her over, but then affected distraction, closing her eyes and with her free hand unclipping her hair, sweeping it back and shaking it out behind her so that her tits quivered invitingly. Her dark Latino nipples were hard and protruding now and gave the lie to her air of casual boredom. As she looked again at me, head tilted sleepily to one side still resting on her hand, she slowly raised one knee, sliding her foot slowly up the lower leg, till it came to rest on the inside of her thigh. Her glistening arousal drew me. I looked and waited still. Her eyes offered…challenged: "Here I am. Look, it's for you… come… take it."

At last without a word but with a slightly trembling hand I unhurriedly took off my shoes and socks and went to her, lying down beside her still in my jeans and t shirt.

"Mmm" she said, breathing heavily now, "A *clothed* boy…you're going to fuck me with your *clothes* on…oh yes…I like that…"

"I'll fuck you any way I like!" I said pulling her roughly to me, and we were unleashed, bodies clashing together launched like sumo wrestlers, ferocious kisses, tongues and legs entwined and hands moving touching grabbing, as if searching for the winning hold.

I felt myself unzipped and her hand unceremoniously pushed inside, fingers curling tight around my cock and yanking it out as mine slid so easily inside her…two…three…frigging her to the knuckles as she worked on me grunting and urging me on.

A minute, two minutes, three…we burst apart, end of round one, gasping for air, taking in great draughts of it. Sian recovered first and grabbed my dick again, sliding down to give it a lick.

"I like it like this," She said, looking, touching…a kiss…a bite…a lingering suck.

"Like what? "I said. "What do you like?"

"I like it sticking out of your jeans…I *like* it!"

Sian just played…it *was* as if she played…like a child with a toy, except *I* was the toy. Minutes sped by and she *played*, intent, fascinated, almost oblivious of *me*, though fully aware too of the effects of her expert attentions. She seemed to know exactly my state of arousal, able to keep me constantly on the brink without bringing me off. I watched her not wanting her to stop…yet… wanting something more…

I tried to push her onto her back but she resisted, and shoved me back hard, raising her leg over me and sliding astride.

"No…no…ME!" she snapped, pushing my shoulders down onto the bed.

"Ok!" I acquiesced, "…Any way you want… have what you want…you always do…I don't care!" And I *didn't* care, just so long as my cock was up Sian's cunt… any way she wanted.

She smiled and leant down to kiss me, a long soft voluptuous kiss.

"Mmmmmmm. I *always* do," she confidently intoned; "But it's so *easy* my darling..." She was drawing back, getting into position... "Because I always..." grabbing my cock and pushing the end firmly into her opening... "Want..."her voice suddenly wavered and she paused a second, fixing me with her gaze, the smile fled and such a look it startled me..."YOU!"

And so saying she he rammed down on me; but the word had erupted from her as a sob, tears suddenly flowing freely as she fucked me, sobbing in small convulsions like a child. Leaning forward her mouth found mine, her face awash with tears, and jumbled garbled words, not even words, grunts...moans... whimpers... unintelligible sounds threaded through urgent desperate kisses, and she shagged me all the while as if our lives depended upon it. I wanted to comfort her, but was so turned on by her fierce metronomic thrusts it was inconceivable that I could stop. Her wild utterances were pushed tongue twisting into my own mouth, lost in her own abandon, and this aroused me even more...and yes so did her visceral distress. What love was this? What anguish?

Our mouths fused, and she gripped my head, fucking me wildly desperately. Her whole body shuddered as she began to come, collapsing down onto me, legs extended as if in some kind of seizure. She was jerking, spasming in a rapid fire of small thrusts, making little high pitched nasal sounds like a small animal. Her mouth was still clamped on mine as if in some strange kiss of life, until the final tremor shook her and she swooned, her head falling to the side as I released with a cry into her, and she wept into my neck.

"Oh my love, my love, my love, my love my love..."

I held her as she wept, limp as a rag doll exhausted, the storm blowing itself out, passing at last. Her breathing eased and like a child she slept. Like a child. I slid myself out from beneath her and gently laid her down. I rose covering her with the duvet, and sat for how long by the window, absently looking at the comings and goings below. My mind was blank. Suddenly I felt like a cigarette.

"Callum."

"You were sleeping."

"Yes. Just…I don't know….hold me?."

I undressed and got into bed, enfolding her, spoons in a drawer.

"Do you want to talk about it?"

She sighed and said nothing.

"What were you trying to say to me?"

"I don't know."

We lay, quiet now, and I waited. At last she turned, her hand lightly caressing my hair, her eyes moist.

"It wasn't meant to be like this. I love you."

"I know."

She kissed me lightly on the lips

"Let's get out of here."

We dressed paid and left, picking up a bottle of wine at the Coop then driving over to Dovestones reservoir. It was midweek and deserted, and we drove up the steep winding water board road to the reservoir on the top at the edge of Saddleworth Moor.

The sun had come out and there was no wind so it was passably warm. I had on a fleece, and Sian fished a pair of flat shoes and a warm jacket from the boot. There was a rug there too, and we headed out a little way onto the moor, finding a sheltered spot to sit and drink the wine in the sunshine.

I realized that a fortnight ago in this situation, after the tears, the reiterated declaration of love, I might well have raised again the question of our future together. Now that was impossible. I wondered if Sian might be expecting me to, hoping I would. I pushed it to one side;

the moment, be in the moment; treasure it; there would not be many left.

Saddleworth Moor is an endless peat wilderness of tough grasses and bog, where even the heather struggles to find a foothold in the black acid earth, exposed in great dark gashes along its flanks. A hard unforgiving place, majestic in its bleakness and scale, but here softened in the sunshine under a cloudless sky, a haven for a while at least. Not for the first time I felt the vastness of the landscape dwarf our difficulties, and it was easy to enjoy the afternoon together with a cacophony of larks singing to us, rising and falling pin pricks high above. Blessed are the birds of the air…

We drank the wine and the landscape moved us to discuss art and artists as we had done many times before. Sian gravitated to what I described as the wild boys, Van Gogh, Turner, Degas, sons of classicism who had spread their wings, Caravaggio with his daring idiosyncratic departures in colour and composition. I bated her that she liked them because they were misfits, rebels, or just downright insane, and provoked her with my not entirely devil's advocate view that Hockney would probably make a better job of this particular landscape than any of the Renaissance or Impressionist big boys. "Come off it darling, it'd end up bright purple. You're just trying to annoy me!"

Sian knew about art, felt it, was passionate about it. We had never been able to go about publicly together in Manchester, to visit a gallery or just go down town. I realized that we quite possibly never would. I suddenly wished I'd had some drawing materials there with me to sketch her. Instead we lolled on the rug, talked and kissed away the afternoon, passing the bottle back and forth. We slipped into heady spiritual and philosophical talk of truth and beauty, human conditioning, relativity and the absolute, for once the physical taking a back seat to metaphysics here in nature, alone in all the world.

Driving back Sian was quiet. Her hand slid across the seat to mine. She glanced at me and smiled.

"You didn't fuck me on the moor." She said, wistfully.

"No."

"But it was lovely."

We drove a little further in silence.

"I like it when you fuck me."

My turn to smile. I was instantly becoming aroused and she knew, her hand diverting to press gently on my erection.

"Will you fuck me now?"

"Yes."

Sian swung the car around at the next junction and we headed back into the wilds. Down a narrow lane we found a small copse, and made love there among the bluebells. We lay supine, her hand in mine, looking up through the trees. The air was still and not a leaf stirred. A blackbird rooted noisily in the leaf litter and was gone. A chaffinch paused to offer a quick burst of song on a branch just above where we lay. Silence then. The distant boring of plane, and we rose together at last without a word to make our way.

Nearing home and our minds were turning to when we might see each other again. Sian suddenly started and put her hand to her mouth with an intake of breath.

"Oh Christ, Callum I forgot! How *could* I have, I'd meant to tell you…a surprise…well, if you can that is…I don't know if you can…Sunday?"

My heart sped up, fearful of what I was about to hear.

"Ray's going to be away all day and overnight. If you could get away we could shoot off to York or Chester or somewhere….have lunch, find an exhibition…I don't know…how are you fixed…have you and Julia got anything on?"

Chapter 29

"I don't think I'm going to come Jules." I'd left it till after dinner, and we were watching the Chanel 4 News.

"What...where?"

"On Sunday, to Stoke, I've been thinking …"

She cut me off, "You've been thinking!?It's arranged, they're expecting us, you've agreed. You've got to come. What the bloody hell are you talking about?"

"I just think you'd be better going on your own. Your Dad'll want to drag me down the pub before lunch, and anyway you want a bit of time with your mum...I just don't see that I need to be there, it's just…"

"It's just supporting me, it's just being with me, it's just doing the fucking decent thing that any partner would do, it's just doing what you said you'd do you shit...don't you bloody dare tell me you're not coming now!"

It was going to be worse than I'd expected, and I had expected it to be bad. Now was the opportunity to recant, to back track, damage limitation and no real harm done. I couldn't.

"Look, Jules…"

"Don't you fucking Jules me! You are the father of my child. We are going to tell the prospective grandparents of the happy event. You have agreed to go and we're going, both of us, end of story!"

"I'm not going Jules."

The silence crackled. Julia sat back in her chair, her thumbnail picking at her fingers, foot twitching like a tiger's tail. She looked at me with a new look that I had not seen on her face before. Alongside Julia's righteous fury she eyed me now with suspicion, uncomprehending disbelief, and faintly pitying disgust. A minute ticked by, maybe two, and it seemed to me that my inability to speak, to produce any semblance of an argument in my defence finally sealed my guilt.

"What's going on Callum?" Julia said, quietly. She waited. I knew that I had to say something, anything to go on the offensive... to be Mr Reasonable and say something appeasing, try to diffuse the situation... anything.

"I just don't want to go." It was all I could manage. I said it knowing it was the wrong thing to say, knowing that even now I could back down and it would blow over and be forgotten. I couldn't.

Julia didn't move. I could hear her breath coming in long tremulous sighs, angry, confused, and thinking back I realize now that she was frightened. I didn't move either. Sitting like a man in the dock, abject, having pled his miserable case, awaiting sentence.

When she spoke again Julia's tone was calm, measured, to all intents and purposes conversational; but there was also an underlying desperation, a dawning realization that all was not well.

"Callum, I'm asking you to come with me to see my parents on Sunday. You agreed to go and I really don't want to go by myself. I *really* want you to come. Maybe it's the hormones, I don't know, but I really want you to be with me, I *need* you to be with me. Please say you're going to come."

I sighed heavily, and saw for a split second a look anticipating relief softening Julia's features. There was still time.

"I'm not coming Jules." My voice, saying words that were mine, but I heard them as if they were spoken by someone else, someone who resembled me but was not.

I felt her eyes on me, cold and cooling, and I looked away, unable to meet her gaze. I heard her rise, and she left the room, quietly closing the door behind her.

Chapter 30

I have wondered if I might have relented had Julia shown her distress more, cried, been depressed and vulnerable. It is hard for me to contemplate that scenario, my pregnant partner struggling and upset, and me selfishly going my own way regardless, not giving a fig. I don't like to think that this could have happened, that I would have been so callous and self-centred, though in all honesty I just don't know. I was on a trip, not in control.

However, this was not how things were, and I was happily relieved of having to witness Julia parading her distress, of having to feel obliged to relent and to support her. Julia did not turn to jelly, but to ice. She became completely self-contained, speaking minimally to me, cool and unfriendly, phoning her friends, returning home from work later on the Thursday after socialising with colleagues. She packed a bag, and told me that she was going to visit a friend in Birmingham on Friday through to Sunday, and would call in to see her parents on the way back.

This let me off the hook, allowing me to conclude that Julia was coping fine. The fact that I had selfishly reneged on an important agreement and very badly let her down could be conveniently put to one side. We had had a row and a fall out followed by a period of the sulks on Julia's part, and we were just 'not speaking.' It was convenient for me to view it this way. It was a situation that made minimal demands of me, a storm that would just blow over if I did nothing.

I would have my all-important time with Sian. I could re-package what happened as a tiff, a major tiff, but none the less just that. I even allowed myself to feel slightly miffed that Julia was being childish and unreasonable. Her pregnancy was the fly in the ointment. This cast me in a light that even then I found uncomfortable. I had to somehow manage to forget about the baby, to write this minor fact out of the script for the present; and this is precisely what I did.

It wasn't so difficult. They say that love is blind. I have to say this is nothing if not an understatement. Love can be the source of creative thinking which may be nothing short of highly delusional; as Paul Simon says in The Boxer, "…a man hears what he wants to hear and he disregards the rest."

It's not a question of there being no inkling, no awareness of what's going on. Reality rumbles along disconcertingly in the background, inescapably uncomfortable, like a mosquito in the room when you are half asleep. We are super selective, however, in what we are prepared to acknowledge, and willing to go through intricate mental distortions to somehow maintain the favoured view of things, the view that facilitates the fulfilment of sexual desire.

What a dangerous game it is! History is littered with famous casualties, and literature celebrates this very thing over and over. Ordinary people living ordinary lives, taken out of themselves and swept into experiences where the super ego is folded neatly into a drawer and put away.ABandoning rational judgement, ruled by physical and emotional gratification, prisoners of the id, blindly courting tragedy, juggling it like the laughing Tom Bombadil did with the One Ring, the ring of power…a dangerous game.

Chapter 31

Sunday arrived. Sian and I made an early start and headed off to York. She wore a blue and white print summer dress with a full skirt, a cropped white cardigan, and white leather heels. "Mmmmmmm very 50's," I said as we pulled away, slipping a hand up her dress, gratified to feel her suspenders completing the 50's theme "Attention to detail too...that's where the devil is!"

Sian slapped my hand away, "Yes, and perhaps 50's courtship rules too young man!"

"OK." I said smoothing her dress back down to her knees as we turned off Barlow Moor Rd onto the start of the M56.

Sian glanced across at me and I smiled. A little further on she glanced across again.

"What's the matter?" I said, and she gave me yet another look... quizzical...miffed?

She slid the car into cruise control.

"I *only* said... 'Perhaps'..."

We were there for lunchtime, and stretched our legs around the old Shambles being tourists for the day, and being free to hold hands, to be out and about together in town, in public doing normal things without fear of being discovered, recognised as cheats. I cannot convey how wonderful this felt. Even here though, we were different... the only tourists *not* taking photographs.

We had an aperitif in a quaint old pub with all the other tourists, and lunched in a posh Italian restaurant by the river, the sun coming out just in time for us to be able to have coffee in the garden. A text came through as we basked soporific in the early spring warmth. It was from Julia: "Helen up 4 w'end. Will stay over & go straight 2 work; back after." Helen was Julia's kid sister, based in London. I smiled and re-read it.

"What are you smiling at…that's an up to no good smile if ever I saw one."

I passed Sian my mobile. "Oh!" She handed it back to me with a look. "Bingo," she softly intoned.

The door had suddenly swung open for us to spend the night together. We savoured the moment, each aware of the others thoughts. She leant across and kissed me.

"I have to be back early for an appointment first thing," she said, "It'll have to be a really early start, unless we just head back later and book in near home?"

"Mmm," I weighed it up. "I don't really fancy the Clarence, do you…not tonight. What if we just tootle over to Wilmslow and find a country place around there somewhere…Alderley Edge maybe?"

I composed a short reply to Julia, but the battery gave out midstream.

"Damn! Phone's gone on the blink. Never mind, she'll not expect a reply."

"Well I won't offer to lend you mine darling…I don't think that would quite do somehow!"

We did the Jorvik, and looked around a couple of small galleries, where I bought an overpriced but very pretty watercolour, a memento of the day for the future. Against all the odds I felt a surge of irrepressible optimism, that there had to be a future for us …somehow…somewhere (yes, I actually thought of the song, casting myself momentarily in West Side Story). My complications, for that's how I neatly thought of them…a kind of technical problem, would be resolved. Love would conquer all. There would be a place for us…

When I'd set out from home that morning it had been with a sense of borrowed time. I was telling myself not to think about it, to enjoy the day. But when it came down to it my problems faded away like a bad dream. When I was with Sian she filled my vision. I've said before how sometimes in intimate moments it felt we were in a bubble with the world going by. Well it was not quite like that, but similar in a way. In York that day we were out and about enjoying doing normal things together and there was no space to consider anything else. Full with each other we were insulated against unwelcome realities. Julia, the baby, the future, it all disappeared. We were together. We were so much in love. Everything would be alright.

This was going to be our first night together, and as well as being an unanticipated gift, in my state of optimistic exuberance it felt like a sort of milestone, not the *only* night, but the *first* one. We were used to grabbing a few passionate hours here and there, but now we were going to be able to have a leisurely dinner after a busy day, to relax and spend the evening together like normal people do. Watch some TV even. It seemed important, this 'normal' thing. Hard to explain, it just did…to me anyway.

We booked into a hotel on the fringe of Alderly Edge in the Cheshire countryside but less than half an hour's drive from home. It was an old timbered coaching house which had been expensively refurbished using lots of wood and opulent drapes and carpets, large sprawling armchairs and couches. The best of the old features had been saved…the grand curved staircase, the bar and some beautiful fireplaces with fires set for the evening. I think many of the doors were original too with new ones carefully matched in, and they had resisted cluttering the space with ad hoc antiques, settling for some tasteful oils and watercolours which drew our attention. It was the sort of place where sounds all seem cushioned to the ear, some decent laid back jazz seeping from somewhere, the staff attentive but unobtrusive.

Our suite was palatial, probably bigger than the flat, and with all the home comforts including a large state of the art TV. We showered and I tried out the technology while Sian was attending to her make up. We were in good spirits. I noticed in the TV schedule that Mastermind was on later on, and I threw down the gauntlet, challenging Sian to compete. She looked momentarily surprised.

"*Mastermind*?"

"Yeah." I smiled. "What's the matter…don't think you're up to it darling?"

"Don't be silly darling…but fine…don't mind… just so long as you feel you'll be able to cope with the disappointment of coming second…!" She turned perplexed back to the mirror.

We had an early dinner and it surpassed expectations. The wine was excellent and we took our time, rounding things off with a Remy and coffee. The ambience was perfect, not many diners but enough, the quiet hum of conversation alongside what I thought to be Chopin's Nocturnes. The lighting was subdued and a log fire flickered in an ornate marble fireplace, attentive waiters gliding back and forth silently on sumptuous carpets.

Returned to our suite I turned down the lights and we sprawled soporific on the couch to watch Mastermind. One of the specialist rounds was on football and I surged ahead, but by the end of the general knowledge was dismally behind and Sian triumphant.

"Never mind darling, you really tried and you did ever so well," she patronized.

"Ha bloody ha," I smarted. "No…never let it be said I'm a bad loser…credit where it's due…you're not just a face…"

"Pathetic…loser!"

There wasn't anything we particularly wanted to watch on the TV, but we continued to watch anyway as you often do, and anyway there was a lingering sense of sticking to the script, snuggled up on the couch together watching TV as *normal* people do. If it seems that I'm overdoing the 'normal' bit slightly, it's because I probably was at the time. It was as if it was some kind of test.

There was a wildlife programme on about elephants. We snuggled. We held hands. We were bored. Sian sighed and I sensed that she was looking at me. I didn't look back, though even this was making me begin to feel turned on, feeling that the 'script' was perhaps about to be shelved.

"Lick me out Callum?"

I turned to look at her.

"Will you lick me out darling?" She said again, matter of fact as if she might have been asking me to pass her the paper.

"OK." I said matter of fact too but immediately excited as I got up to turn the TV off. "I'll put the lights on," I said and went to do so, Sian now standing too and taking her knickers off.

"Shall I take my stockings off?" she said over her shoulder.

"Oh no, leave them on…just the way you are…well…maybe you could put your shoes on?"

Sian was smiling at this as she sat back down on the couch and slipped on her heels. I was standing a little way in front of her, and for a second she sat demurely, legs together, smoothing her hair back. Then without any more ado she lay back and slid her bum over the edge, opening her knees wide apart, feet planted firmly on the floor. Her dress was hitched up to her waist.

"You see Callum," she said as I took in her spread thighs and her cunt, boldly, unashamedly presented for me, "I'm not just a pretty face…"

"I love it." I said.

With utter simplicity she replied, "It's me. Kiss me. Love me."

This said it all. Our love…our sex…it was who we were, overwhelming, not to be denied. It was a love of outrageous candidness, unabashed pleasure-seeking, rejoicing in each other's bodies. It was not *just* sex, but pure absolute sex, sex cubed, raised to another level. We were man and woman completely surrendered one to the other, exploring with such confidence and boundless joy the gifts we brought… open access…

"Kiss *me*," she whispered.

I knelt and kissed her cunt. I kissed it just in the same way I so often kissed her lips; a flurry of small tender kisses, turning to kiss her soft inner thighs just as I kissed her cheeks, returning to her cunt, a soft pliant snog, flittering my tongue tentatively around the lips, and more small kisses, just a little more insistent now encouraged by Sian's soft moans. She returned my cunt-kisses, pushing forward to meet my lips. I turned again to kiss her thighs, to lick, to bite as I would her neck. Her breathing was heavier now and hands firmly on my head trying to gently turn me back to where she most wanted me to be, tilting up for more…

I paused, enjoying her small impatient movements as she waited. A tentative lick, running the very tip of my tongue up her slit, and at last I buried my face between her legs plunging my tongue into her hole, drinking deep. French kisses now, and Sian was sighing ecstatically, "Oh…Oh…up me… UP ME…*YES*! It's all for you, my love…take it!"

I pushed my tongue deep, rubbed my face against her, bathing in her pungent juices. She tasted wonderful and my face was soaked, snogging her passionately now. She had raised her knees up into the air above my shoulders and I'd wrapped my arms tight around her supporting her in a loving embrace. And so we kissed…this was how we kissed.

We kissed like this for a long time. My hair was darkened with her juices and my T-shirt stained wet. I paused to get my breath, but Sian had other ideas. Reaching down she deftly opened her slit with two fingers, grabbed my head and pulled me hard onto her clit, nestled protruding there like a small nipple, waiting to be sucked, *demanding* to be sucked.

I tongued and sucked it for all I was worth, and felt Sian move into another gear. She gripped my head with her thighs frantically forcing my mouth hard against her, tilting rhythmically with small staccato cries. She didn't take long to come, no ceremony now just shagging my face in small hard jerks, coming with a long cry, her movements lengthening, slowing, moaning loud and long, gripping me like a vice. I could barely breathe, and momentarily thought this might be one of the better ways to go…wondered if she could feel my involuntary smile! She trembled on my lips, shuddered, and was spent.

We rested as we were, my cheek pressed against her cunt, breathing in great draughts of air, her fingers lightly stroking my hair.

"Oh Callum…Oh Callum…" was all that she said.

I think she may even have slept very briefly, and I waited, quietly…time for everything…

"Now you." She whispered at last. "Take off your clothes."

I stood up and took off my T-shirt, unbuckled my belt and pushed my jeans and underpants down in one. My erection had subsided but sprung back even as my jeans came down and Sian leaned forward immediately to take it in her mouth. She took it deep and bit on the shaft till I winced, then firmly encased the knob in her mouth, sucking and running her tongue around it, hands on my bum and nails digging, digging.

We changed places and as I kicked off my jeans her dress came over her head and she unhooked her bra. "Stockings?"

"On."

She smiled and knelt between my legs, continuing the theme... kissing, kissing everywhere... my thighs, stomach, balls ...licking, biting, sucking, and pulling on my cock, taking my balls in her mouth, her tongue pushing softly against them as she wanked me. I was near.

"Don't bring me off." I gasped.

"No," she said, coming up now, "Don't worry...I *am* going to fuck you."

She sat by me and we kissed, long and loving. She paused and cupped my face, slipped her tongue into my mouth again, then held me there, her gaze unsure...ambivalent...challenging but frightened at the same time, undecided whether to mock me or weep: "Do you love me?"

"Yes."

"Do you want me?"

"Yes."

She kissed me again, still holding my face in her hands.

"More than anything?"

"Yes."

It was true.

She smiled then, an indulgent collusive smile. She had me slide right down as she had been before when I licked her out. Facing away from me she stood astride my legs bending forward. Her hand snaked through between her legs to grasp my cock and I watched as she very slowly lowered herself, watched my dick disappear up her lovely cunt. She flexed her knees and began to fuck me. Her hands braced on my knees steadied and supported her and I watched mesmerized as my cock slid in and out of her, her bum, her whole body rising and falling, impaling herself as she fucked me.

I watched her rising and falling, flexing from the knees, her back beginning to shine with sweat as she rode me. I grabbed her arse, squeezed and kneaded her buttocks, pulling her cheeks apart, pressing my thumb against her bum.

"Oh yes...YES!" she exclaimed loudly and froze, panting hard with the exertion, bent over, poised on the end of my dick...waiting. I wet my forefinger and slid it a little way into her bum. She gasped, tensed for a long second or two, then easing back onto my cock she took my finger to the knuckle up her bum.

"Yes... oh yes!" she gasped again, pushing down and wriggling, sitting back now, her back straight. "Fucking hell...fucking hell...oh god!" she whispered to herself. I could feel her trembling.

At last she leant forward pushing down with her hands on my knees and I held my own hand steady as she resumed fucking me, ramming herself down again and again with loud grunts onto my dick and finger both. I watched her shagging me, transfixed and trembling now too, overtaken by a febrile excitement observing our own fell coupling like an out of body experience, but one which was *only* body, oblivious now to who this woman was...who *I* was, only the sex, the bodies, colliding, fused, ecstatic... beyond ourselves.

The effort for Sian was taking its toll. She was sweating and her breathing was laboured, but I knew that we were both very near. I called out to her... god knows what...and she seemed to summon a last effort to ram down on me once...twice...three times. Her sphincter tightened like a vice around my finger as she came and I shot my spunk into her, trembling, wave after wave. She grabbed my hand yanking my finger out of her bum and sitting straight backed, writhing and grinding on my cock, groaning, lost in her own orgasm. I leaned forward to hold her, cupping her tits, my cheek slipping against the sweat on her back, as at last she slumped into me, collapsed, still joined.

We showered together and sent down for a bottle of champagne, listened to music and talked, having giggling donned the fluffy hotel bathrobes AND slippers! It had been a long day, and when we found our way to bed we were both all in, as well as being somewhat the worse for wear with the champers bottle dutifully upturned in the bucket.

Sian was in my arms and raised her head from my chest to plant a kiss lightly on my lips.

"I love you Callum." She snuggled in again. "It was lovely earlier…with your finger and everything."

"Mmmmmmm." I kissed her hair. "I know you like it…I had an amazing view!" My cock was twitching against her thigh and she lightly ran her nails along its length, smiling at my sharp intake of breath

"I thought you *might* have been going to fuck me up the bum…" She kissed me again with a little flitter of her tongue, a fleeting flash of her eyes… and turned over onto her side.

To wake in the early morning with my lover, the first light filtering through the curtains and the dawn chorus already underway. I surfaced briefly from sleep, to feel her arm slung loosely across my body, her leg over mine, her breath so close. I kissed her and her eyes flickered open and met mine with a sleepy smile.

"I love you," she whispered, her eyelids fluttering closed, slipping back into the gentle meandering flow of sleep.

"Would you like some breakfast?" This time it was I who was awakened with a kiss. Sian's head was on my chest, her hand squeezing my dick. I glanced at my watch; six a.m.

"Oh it's too early yet...Sian..." I whinged as she pulled the duvet aside; but she wasn't getting up...she was turning round into sixty-nine.

"Mmmmmmm breakfast..." she said, licking my cock and taking it in her mouth. She nudged my lips with her soft insistent cunt. I nuzzled it, smelled her, already wet, and ripe from the night before.

"Cock milk for me... cunt juice for Callum..." she recited playfully as if ordering from the menu, beginning to suck and pull in earnest now, as my tongue pushed into her slit, and deeper into her hole.

I thumbed her clit as I licked and probed, and she came quickly, and had come again shuddering and biting on my cock by the time I felt my spunk beginning to rise and explode pumping into her mouth. She froze, her lips clamped on my shaft, my balls cupped in her hand; still now, receiving my semen until it was spent, then sharing it with me in a lingering flooded kiss; our tongues turning against each other as we tasted then drank, locked together, indivisible, one.

It was very early but we had to move. We were the first to breakfast and together quietly made our start to the day. It had been our first night together. What joy! We were replete.

Chapter 32

It was still early when Sian dropped me off. We kissed and parted brightly, full of warmth and well-being. She seemed so happy, and I felt confident...all would be well.

I had barely walked through the door when the phone rang. As I went to pick it up I noticed six messages showing on the display, and was already thinking excuses. It was Helen:

"Callum its Helen. For Christ's sake where've you been, I've been phoning you half the night!"

"Oh god, sorry...I've just come down...took a sleeping pill...I haven't been...what's the matter?"

"Oh Callum, its Julia..." she ground to a momentary halt and I froze, a sinking feeling suddenly dragging at my innards.

"What?! Helen? For god's sake is she alright?"

"Yes, yes" she rushed on, "She's fine...just a few bruises...cracked ribs...it was a car...drunk....hit us on the way home....she hadn't put her seatbelt on....she's....she's....oh Callum!" She tailed off.

"Look Helen, just be calm, take a deep breath....she's OK, that's the main thing...are *you* OK? Where is she now?"

"Yes I'm fine...I had mine on...Oh Callum, she's lost the baby!"

Silence; Helen crying; my mind stunned, not computing, the information unreceived.

"What? I don't understand."

Helen paused, gathering herself, calmer now.

"Callum, Julia's had a miscarriage. They've kept her in...she's in hospital...Stoke Royal, ward four. Callum? Callum... are you there?"

Once again I heard my voice as if from another person, somebody else, beyond me, not me.

"Yes…sorry Helen, I was just…thanks, I'll be there as soon as I can."

Helen talked on, reassuring, practical, obviously sensing my shock and distress and rallying to offer support.

I put down the phone. Julia was alright. I said it out loud. She was alright. Thank God. But the baby, gone before begun, my happy blooming mother-to-be, robbed of her joy, whilst I was…I could not bear the thought. I visualized her in her hospital bed, bruised and bereft, alone; poor Helen, their parents, a world out there from which I had become estranged. I saw myself, stunted and withered; such cruelty, such loss; and yet a small shoot had broken through my burnt and barren ground, and I breathed.

Something opened, and incredibly amid the debris I found strength and purpose springing from a new feeling, one which I had forgotten…empathy, compassion. I checked the trains, put my mobile on charge, and began to gather the necessaries for a short trip. I phoned the hospital and was told Julia was fine, but they were being cautious, keeping her in till tomorrow. I could go anytime.

I steeled myself and phoned Julia on her mobile. I heard her voice and it just flowed out:

"Jules, it's me. Oh God Jules, I'm so sorry…Jules, I'm so sorry…please….Jules…are you OK…I mean, I know, how can you be? I'm so sorry." I was crying now but tried to continue… "I didn't get the messages…I was…"

She interjected as I stumbled, not sure in any case what I was going to say.

"Shhhh, it's Ok, Helen phoned, she told me…you took one of your damn pills. Oh Callum, I don't know what to do!"

She was crying now, little childlike sobs.

"I'm coming down Jules…the 11-30 train…I should have been there…it would never have happened. I can't tell you how sorry I am my love. Oh my god, what have I done?!"

There was a snuffling silence on the other end of the phone.

"I need you Callum, come soon my love. Don't worry. It's not your fault…just one of those things. A bigger one than most," she laughed bitterly, "but not your fault, not anybody's. I should have had my bloody seatbelt on."

"No! Don't say that… no regrets, there's no blame Jules…do you hear!? We have each other. This is just something that… has happened… a terrible, terrible something! Just hang in. I'll be strong for us, I'll be with you…I *am* with you!"

"Thank you. I love you."

Her words hung in the air like damnation, generous beyond anything I deserved, a stiletto unwittingly eased into my heart; but I was not going to capitulate to wretchedness now, not now. It was over. I had to look beyond myself, to my sad hurt woman who I had betrayed, and to my lost child.

"I love you Julia. You hang in till I get there. It'll be alright. Try to get some sleep."

Chapter 33

As I sat on the 11-30 train out of Piccadilly, I observed the people, the colours, heard snippets of conversation, gazed at the suburbs then the countryside passing by. It all seemed new. The proverbial scales had dropped from my eyes and I could see again.

I would not say that there was no backward glance; that would not be true. The day before was fresh in my mind and when I thought of it, of Sian, I felt sad, wondered what might have been...even then felt a pang of desire. Yet it occurred to me that she would not suffer as much as I would have done had she ended the affair. Why did I think this? She loved me, but was not lost in this love as I had been, rudderless and hardly able to function normally, possessed. I realized that for Sian I was a part of her life, but not all of it; we had something special, something vibrant and exciting, intoxicating even, but Sian had a perspective on it that I did not have, and it was always I who had attempted to push it forward and for us to be together. And even as I thought about our wonderful wonderful sex, I thought of how we were not able to snuggle up together contentedly to watch TV. A small thing yet it had bothered me slightly at the time, and now I thought I understood.

I could see this now, love rooted in desire, single faceted in it's intensity; but even as I considered this and my new found path, I felt a stab of longing, and openly questioned to myself whether I could see things through, resist returning for more, put aside my dream of a life with this woman. We only have one life, and the stark fact remained, there was no baby now, and yet ironically the tragic removal of this insurmountable obstacle saw me abandoning my dream rather than pursuing it. There were doubts. I had come to mistrust my judgement, to know my frailty. It was the resolve of the addict.

I thought about Julia, this woman who seemed to have always been a part of my life, and who I had so abused. I knew that what I was doing was not simply atonement. I had realized that I really could not envisage my life without her. When Helen had hesitated I had momentarily thought that she was going to tell me that there had been a tragic accident and that Julia was dead. The reality awful as it was, came to me with a sense of relief, and shattered the carapace that had built up around me. Corny as it sounds, I had indeed seen the light, and knew what I must do. I did not doubt that it was the right path, but did doubt myself; I had become a close friend of desire; I knew her well, alas as she did me.

I must sound as if I was quite half-hearted, not entirely convinced, liable to fall by the wayside and already anticipating it. Well that isn't the way it was. I was simply and perhaps for me unusually (unaccustomed as I was) acknowledging the truth, my weakness which had become my shame, and which I had to be aware of if the better part of me was to prevail.

I was so looking forward to seeing Julia, to caring for her, to helping her through her awful loss. To try to share it with her and shoulder some of the burden was all that I wanted to do. It seems a long time ago now, but I can remember very well the feeling of warmth, that I had found something good, something right. I felt certain in my path, confident in my decision, hopeful that I could, would see this through and not deviate once things returned to normal. No longer the ducking diving dissembler I had become, I felt renewed, revived, and I will say it, redeemed.

A strange word that jars a little in the context of modern parlance, but that's how it felt; it's the right word for the way I felt... that day... on the train. I have thought about this notion of redemption. There has to be a quid pro quo. For me the loss of our child was the awful down payment on my redemption, this and the dreadful realisation that I might have lost Julia too.

Yes there was atonement...simple guilt and restitution. But redemption is quite different to simply changing course, putting one's house in order, putting things right. It is literally being saved and renewed...the ultimate catharsis. Christ the redeemer is also known as the saviour. This might seem to imply that this is a process that happens *to* you, a sort of conversion, a response to events which involves certain realizations and changes. All these things may occur, but essentially redemption is being saved, and the notion that this can happen from without, that it is as it were simply a response to events, is insufficient. It is much more.

I was changed, and experienced a clarity which was in such contrast to the murky confusion of the past year. I was acknowledging my love for Julia, treasuring it, and this was at the core of my transformation. Yet in all the past year my many declarations of love had been made to another woman, to Sian, even as recently as the day before, fully committed to and believed...and not entirely disowned even now! But something *had* shifted. I *knew* what I had to do, without the need to understand it all, to tease out the tangled threads.

Perhaps I *had* mistaken desire... passion, for love, and been swept away by a sexual tidal wave. I would not have been the first and wouldn't be the last. That is what most people would say. But whilst with hindsight I can see how there might be something in this, I have wondered at the sheer power of what I experienced. You see, even now I don't know. What I knew then was that I had emerged from a state of confusion and deep unhappiness where I had been lost, where I had pawned my soul for a physical and emotional high. I had been trapped in the turbulence of desire, an endless round of longing, 'lost in love'. But was it really a forgery? It was beautiful, and I was seared by the flame. Was this really counterfeit goods? I could not say. What is true and what is not? But walking out of that place, I could see again, I could breath, I was free, and my choice was so easy... this at least was true.

None of this was in my mind that day. In fact I probably would have simply said I loved both women in different ways, but Julia was my soul-mate, and I could not bear to lose her, so my path was clear. I was still a frail divided soul, and unsure of many things except that is for one: as the train sped me to Stoke to be with Julia, my Jules, who I loved and had so nearly lost, I knew I had been saved.

Chapter 34

Julia was sitting on a chair by the side of her bed when I arrived, her pen in her mouth, staring blankly at the crossword. It's funny how in hospital you always expect patients to be propped up on pillows in bed, even if they're just in for tests or ingrowing toenails. She didn't notice me immediately, and I wondered for a second if she had dozed off in the chair. Her face was badly bruised; two black eyes and a very puffy nose.

I'd intended to say something funny, light, the old me, the old her, a little banter to ease the way. All I could manage was her name. "Jules," I said quietly, clutching the bunch of tulips I'd bought at a garage.

She looked up, eyes blank for the split second it took to come back from wherever she had been to register my presence with a twinkle of delight, jumping to her feet and throwing her arms around my neck, narrowly avoiding squashing the flowers.

"Oh Callum, I'm so glad you're here!" She hugged me close and I kissed her hair, but then winced and let out a little gasp as I squeezed her, "Careful...ribs are a bit..."

"Sorry," I said. "Yes," dropping the flowers onto the bed and taking her hands, "I'm here. "

She kissed me and looked at me. "I'm a bit of a mess."

"Yes," I said.

Julia threaded the tulips among some carnations in a vase and climbed onto the bed and I occupied her seat. We looked at the effect. "Very...erm..."

"Yes, very!"

I cast an eye over her long flannelette nighty, white and covered in tiny pink flowers, Peter Pan collar and all, "...and the nighty...very..."

"Oh definitely...*very*...my mums."

"How are you Jules?"

"Oh, just a couple of cracked ribs...and this," she said pointing to her face. "Idiot pulled out without stopping, right in front of us. It must've been the steering wheel did the damage. Stupid me hadn't put on my seatbelt. We'd just been to the local...could have walked really only it was raining..."

Her voice wobbled and I interrupted, taking her hand, "How are you Jules?"

She sighed, a long deep sigh.

"Oh, you know, empty I suppose..." but starting to cry even as she emitted a little bitter laugh at her bad joke.

I squeezed her hand and let her cry, silently, wiping her eyes with the sleeve of her nighty, "It was our one chance Callum. I fluffed it."

"No you didn't. Something happened, that's all. Things happen. You can't stop things happening Jules. I should've been there, then it might not have happened that way. We might not have taken the car....or *I* might have been driving, much faster than you and both of us killed...things happen."

We were quiet for a minute.

"When can you come home?"

"Oh, maybe today, but probably tomorrow after the doctor's ward round. I don't mind in a way; just giving me time to adjust, to take it in."

"I'll look after you."

"Yes, I know."

"You'll be off for a bit."

"Yeah; they won't want me cluttering up the place looking like this. Still, I can get on with some stuff at home, I'd rather keep busy...you know..."

"Yeah, I suppose. We can get online and book Cordoba."

"Yeah, let's do that," she said, trying to raise some enthusiasm in her voice. "You'll stay over at my parents? They'll be very offended if you don't, anyway Helen's still there so it won't be too bad!"

"I guess so," I said, "You'd better give me the number…I'll put it in my phone now."

It was oppressively warm, and I took of my Jacket and slung it on the back of the chair. "Come on then, crossword…let the dog see the rabbit!"

We managed most of it between us, and it was a nice, neutral thing to do, not avoiding the elephant in the room, but allowing ourselves time just to *be* together, reconnecting. There was time enough for talking, for sharing the load, working through.

I went off to find a loo and to fetch a couple of coffees from the café, realizing that this was the first time in a very long time that I had felt calm and content, at ease with myself and the world around me. Navigating the hospital took a while. When I returned Julia's eyes were closed, though she was sitting up with her mobile in her hand and obviously not asleep. I thought she couldn't have heard my approach and announced, "Coffee for Madame" as I deposited the drinks on the bedside cabinet. Julia didn't stir, and it was then that I noticed how pale she was, and simultaneously that it was not *her* mobile that she held, but mine.

"Oh God…Jules…please…" I reached for the phone but she snatched it away with a look of pure venom.

"Jules, please…don't…" but she tapped at the keypad and a voice came through on speaker:

"Hello darling, I hope I didn't tire you out yesterday. It was wonderful. I can't wait till Wednesday. I've bought some very small things to hardly wear! I know you like skimpy…hope you like red. I love you…"

"Jules, it was over as soon as I heard…it *is*…over…she doesn't know yet. Jules…oh god, please, please…"

I tried to take her hand but she flinched away.

"How long?"

"About a year," I murmured, my voice breaking. I cleared my throat, "About a year," I repeated quietly, "I've been out of my mind, please listen, let me…"

"Get out," she whispered.

"Jules it's over, I'm so sorry…please don't…"

"GET OUT!" she shouted now "GET OUT!" flinging the phone at me hugging her knees and sobbing convulsively into the flannelette as I begged incoherently to be allowed to stay, trying to hold her as she flailed at me screaming over and over, "GET OUT! GET OUT..!"

Several nurses arrived at once, two tending Julia now wailing like a child, as the others picked up my phone and jacket, ushering me out of the ward calling out to her, her sobs tearing at my heart, knowing it was over.

Chapter 35

On the train heading home I was stunned, in a state of shock. In the course of less than a day my life had resurged, had moved as I saw it from the darkness into the light, and then had crumbled into ruin. It was difficult to think at all, and yet I knew that I must. The instinct to survive struggled with something much darker. Could I go on…did I *want* to go on…did I *have* to? Was it futile self-delusion to think that anything could come from all this that would make life worth living. I thought of the stock market term "the dead cat bounce," the tendency for a large drop in a share price to be followed by a very small and short lived bounce, as with a dead cat dropped from a high building. It was considerably more than I could now envisage for myself. It was the end.

The finality of what had happened was absolutely clear. There was no way back from this situation with Julia, and I knew this. Julia was not a desperate needy person. She was in dire straits, but she was a capable woman, a person of substance who would back her own ability to rebuild her life. My duplicity on the day of her miscarriage, graphically announced as I tendered my love and devotion by her hospital bed, left not the slightest possibility of forgiveness. As I began to pick through the rubble this stark fact provided a wall behind me, if not a floor beneath my feet. There was no need to consider whether or how reconciliation might be pursued. It also made it doubly futile to dwell on the awful manner of my fall from grace. There was no way back.

The full realization slowly took form emerging from the smoke of destruction like Banquo's ghost. It was a little like the realization following the death of a loved one that you will never ever see that person again… not immediate…hard beyond measure to accept, but insistent on being accepted too, so that you may then focus, grieve, move on. As the train rattled on like a cattle truck to hell I saw this was the case, beyond doubt, beyond hope, and the shrivelling pain provided me with an end from which I might begin.

Whether to begin was another matter. My life had convulsed. I was able to see myself through Julia's eyes and feel her loathing and what's more knew that it was deserved, no place lower to fall. To end it would be to do the honourable thing.

Such things passed through my mind, but simultaneously I was already examining the debris, looking for a reason to live, frightened, jostled along by the imperative of survival. I wonder whether all potential suicides go through this process first, scanning their lives for one half realistic repository for hope, one good reason *not* to take their lives. There was a balance to be struck between the fear and finality, of the practically easy route and the hardship of struggling through in abject misery without any real belief that the outlook would improve, that it would be worth it. Perhaps the act itself of looking for a shred of hope makes the difference between those who will end their lives and those who briefly contemplate it but will not, and the ultimate act indeed follows hard upon the heels of the abandonment of hope.

Yesterday I had yearned to have the possibility of a future with Sian, but today had discounted this for the genuine, authentic, 'wholesome' love that I recognised in my relationship with Julia, a relationship in which I could live and grow. By implication my relationship with Sian was of a lesser order, insubstantial, a costly indulgence responsible for my demise. I had to a some extent acknowledged this, made my choice, even congratulated myself on having achieved a degree of wisdom and seen it for what it was.

I replayed in my mind the voicemail message from Sian, but listened to it with Julia's ears… red skimpy underwear… and I had betrayed Julia and our unborn child, lost everything. How pathetic. The somersaults required for me to turn the clock back to yesterday were surely impossible even for me.

Yet I had nothing. It came down to this; and Sian was still there, no impediment now… if there was the will. If I had not the courage to die, I had somehow to go on. I was alone, and desolate beyond words. Ray would soon know about us, of that I was sure. Julia would not spare Sian in that. Sian may very soon be free, albeit in a way she had never expected to be. I saw here the faintest chink of light, and ran toward it. Going back was not a possibility, but going forward, bringing this 'affair' into the open, taking Sian with me, building a life together…

The train was approaching Piccadilly. There was a straw and I was already reaching for it, like a man on death row seeking a reprieve.

Chapter 36

I arrived home to find a message on the ansafone. It was Julia, icy, asking that I leave before her return at the weekend. She was going to have the flat valued and engage a solicitor to sort out division of the equity, hoping to be in a position to buy me out. She asked that I appoint a solicitor also, and let her know their details, but not to attempt to speak to her.

It was not unexpected, though the swiftness with which she had rallied to deliver this ultimatum took me by surprise, and hearing it said was hard, nailing the lid on the coffin firmly shut. It was early evening. I e-mailed Sian and texted too, asking her to come round as soon as. I was in luck. She'd picked up the text and the urgency, texting back to say she was coming over.

When the doorbell rang I started as if it was a gun shot. My nerves were frayed. My fate was in the balance with this one interview, a last chance. The door closed and she was in my arms, her familiar scent, hair soft against my face, those lips... I felt the familiar rush of love and affection cushioning the traumas of the last twenty four hours. All may yet be well.

"What is it darling? You look awful. Has something happened?" She was looking at me now, concerned, evidently alarmed at my urgent summons.

"Yeah, you could say that, come in...drink?...have one, you'll need it." I poured two stiff scotches and we sat.

"Julia and I...it's over." Now she was alarmed.

"What?! How? Callum what's happened...where is she?"

"She's at her parents, back at the weekend. I'll be moving out." The look of alarm deepened.

"But how? Can you not patch it up? What's happened?"

"She knows Sian...about us. I had to go down there to see her today. She was in hospital...they tried to get me last night..."

"Oh God we were..."

"Yes, we were."

"But is she OK? Why's she in hospital? You didn't tell her did you?"

I sank the scotch and poured another. "She's OK. A car pulled out in front of hers and she hit it...just a few bruises, cracked ribs. She was pregnant Sian, one in a million chance. She miscarried...lost the baby."

"Oh my God."

We sat in silence. Sian finished her scotch and waved the offered bottle away.

"Poor Julia. Poor you. I'm really sorry Callum. But how did she find out...about us?"

I took out my mobile. "I'd left it in my jacket pocket in the hospital when I went to get us some coffees. Nobody phones me much...she got curious."

I played the message.

"Oh my God. I think I *will* have that drink."

I steadied myself. It had to be now. Sian offered the opening. "What are you going to do?"

I moved beside her on the couch and took her hand. "I want us to be together...now. It's time Sian...it'll soon be out. Stay here tonight. We'll tell Ray in the morning."

I wasn't prepared for the look. She was aghast. "You can't be serious," she said stiffly, withdrawing her hand, straightening her posture, formal and cool now. "Callum I'm really sorry for you and Julia, but surely you don't expect me to leave Ray because *your* relationship has ended?"

I shifted uneasily in my seat. I hadn't expected such a forthright and unequivocal response. "Of course not… not because of our breakup, but because it's the right time, don't you see?"

"The right time for what? What *are* you talking about Callum?" Now she was being obtuse. I felt my frustration rising and my hopes sliding away. I tried to appear calm, but realized I was swimming against the tide, and my voice shook.

"Look Sian, we love each other…" I dried up. Sian's expression was implacable, her demeanour cool and hostile. I felt my words breaking on her stony ground.

"Callum," she enunciated calmly but very assertively, " Ray and I are together. We are **not** going to part. I'm really sorry for what's happened to you, but I can't help that, and you really can't expect me to follow suit."

I could no longer hold myself in check, "Oh for Christ's sake Sian stop this! You love me! You've told me a thousand times. We've talked about this before. Christ you don't even sleep with Ray…waiting for him to take off with his woman. What do you think's going to happen when he finds out? Do you think Julia's going to spare your sensitivities? You have to…"

"Ray already knows." She whipped out, interrupting my desperate tirade. I thought I must have misheard.

 "What?" I said. "What did you say?"

"Ray already knows Callum, he's known for quite some time."

I slumped back in the cushions. The seconds ticked by. "But he can't…he would've…that time at football…"

"Callum, he knows. He didn't know then…that it was you… just that I had a man (that had been agreed) but he guessed, after your conversation with him. He asked me and I told him. You gave it away with whatever you said about 'visuals.' Ray's very sharp Callum. He didn't mind…he doesn't mind, he thinks it's…" she tailed off.

"Thinks it's what?"

"He thinks it's funny, or at least he did. Lately he's been worried about you."

My head was spinning. "Just a minute, just a minute, let me get this straight. Ray and you had agreed that you could have sex with someone else, *were* having sex with someone else, he finds out it's me, and that's…all OK? What the fuck's all this about Sian?"

Sian sat back in her seat and closed her eyes for a second. "Callum, when I said Ray and I are together, I was conveying that we are really together. We understand one another…deeply. We have agreed that each of us can have someone else. It's…interesting, we like it. It's something we do."

It was cool, matter of fact. I barely recognised her. "But…you said you didn't even sleep with him…you swore it sobbed it…begged me to believe you; and all those times you've said you loved me, wept as we made love…you meant it…I felt it."

"Ray was spoiling that time at Henry's. It was mischief. I said what I had to in order to keep you. You were better than the others Callum," she softened, putting her hand on mine, "You were special, on my wave length, a great fuck. I didn't want to lose you."

She paused, grinding to a halt. I said nothing, stunned, and she sighed, removing her hand and looking at her watch. I realized she was about to leave, yet still could not let go.

"Sian, why would you tell me you loved me? Why *did* you tell me you loved me…wanted to be with me?" I said it quietly, still disbelieving that she had not meant the things she said, grasping at a straw that she may yet recant upon her denial.

Sian sighed again, and her growing impatience showed. "I just *did*. I don't know why…probably because…because *you* did. I hadn't expected you to get so serious, just to have some fun; but then it was all so nice, so romantic… it made sex better…we fucked like we meant it, we *really* made love. I got into it…I mean I did…I really did love you…at the time…each time… just… not… *all* the time. I never thought that you *really* believed it. I mean…oh for Christ's sake! I'm sorry Callum. It's been a lot of fun."

A great fuck; a lot of fun; how gullible, how demeaned I was, and I remembered how Ray had warned me. But now as the sandcastle slipped into the sea and I heard the past tense running through Sian's last sentence, I was overtaken by panic, my dignity finally slipping away with my foolish dreams. She was rising to go and I stood up quickly with her.

"Look, it's alright…I mean…it's alright…don't worry…darling…I understand…it's fine." I stammered, trying to lighten my voice, even to smile, collusive, worldly, god knows what. Sian looked bemused.

 "Sorry, what's alright? I'm not with you?"

"You…and Ray…well it's a bit of a shock but it's OK…it's cool."

"I have to go Callum."

"Yeah… sure…of course…so…Wednesday…the Clarence…are you going to pick me up?"

 Astonishment, but something else…a flicker of amusement…an eyebrow slightly raised… quizzical.

 "Goodbye Callum." She turned her back and was gone.

Chapter 37

I was calm. It was over. I poured another drink. There was no intention formed, no decision; just another drink; alone now; the end. Things would take their course. After all the struggle, the confusion, the fear, there was peace.

It must have been very late by the time I made my way to Parrs Wood railway station. It was a long walk, quiet, nobody about, and a fine crisp night. I remember humming as I strolled along, 'Ricky don't lose that number,' smiling, happy to feel that all that was behind me now.

I'd written a note for Julia, just saying sorry, that she'd done the right thing, what anyone would have done, that she deserved and would get better than I had managed to give her...that it was time for me to go. I'd struggled over the note. I knew my death would hurt her, of course, but could not leave without saying goodbye, making my peace.

Parrs Wood is a small local station, and at that time of night it was deserted. I ascended the ramp to the platform and climbed down onto the track, walked a little way along the line. There was a bright moon, almost full, lending a chill ghostly clarity to this deserted place, silvering the surface of the track stretched out before me like Jacob's ladder. All was silent save my own footfall, and my cold-cast shadow went before me. Such peace. All *was* well...at last.

I carefully made my way, counting the sleepers, for some reason having decided on fifty as the place where I would stop. I took off my fleece and made a pillow of sorts, put my head on the rail, and quickly fell asleep as a taxi rattled by under the bridge, and the silent night closed about me once more.

I hadn't noticed the police car parked up off Wilmslow Road. The lights must have been off. It was probably an afterthought that he'd belatedly decided to follow me up the station ramp. Perhaps things were slack, a Monday night, his radio unusually quiet.

At any rate, I was fast asleep when I felt a hand on my shoulder rousing me, and woke up to the glare of a torch shining in my face. A police woman stood to one side. "What's your name son," he said as I shielded my face from the glare.

"Callum."

"What you doing here Callum?"

"Waiting for a train," I said, not intending it as a joke; he realized that but laughed anyway.

"Come on then lad, let's be having you." I didn't move.

"I haven't finished yet."

"I'm afraid you have Callum. Come on. You've had a few haven't you? You'll thank me tomorrow."

"No I won't. "

"Oh I think you will."

"No I won't."

"Yes you will."

"No I won't."

"Will a thousand times! Come on, on your feet before my bollocks freeze off." I didn't move and the WPC interjected:

"Have a fag Reg, let me have a word."

"All yours," he said, "But before the next train if you can…"

She sat on the line next to me. "What's up Callum?"

"Life."

"Yeah," She said, "It's a bitch…and then you die."

I turned my head to look up at her, "So let me do *my* bit."

"Sorry Callum not on my shift; and Reg is right, you'll thank us tomorrow."

"No I won't."

"Yes you…" she broke off and laughed. "Come on Callum, there'll be a train along soon and I'm not leaving you here. You wouldn't want to get an innocent young policewoman killed now would you?"

She looked nice…kind. "Are you innocent?" I said.

"No, but that's what I like to tell people." She smoothed my hair and placed her hand under my upper arm. "Come on love."

I rose unsteadily stiff and full of scotch. "I need a pee."

Reg was back and they both laughed now, linking an arm each likes pals on a night out. "Aye… well… let's just get off the tracks first," he said.

Descending from the dark deserted station to the brightly lit road I did not feel saved, but rather the most profound sense of loss. I was crying now, silently, as they helped me into the car. It was ended, and now it was all beginning again. Reg drove as the kind policewoman radioed base to alert the hospital that we were on our way.

Chapter 38

The mention of hospital had jolted me. It was not the casualty department they were taking me to. As the police car purred through the empty streets I grappled with myself to take stock of my situation, which felt suddenly more serious than when my head was on the railway line.

I knew nothing about psychiatric hospitals except for what I had seen in the movies and on television. 'One Flew Over The Cuckoo's nest' came back to me and I recalled the message that had the most immediate bearing on my current predicament...that those considered risky/dangerous would be held against their will until the authorities deemed it safe to let them go. Here I was, heading for a psychiatric ward in a police car having been found with my head on a railway line, and having clearly admitted my suicidal intentions to a policewoman. Shit.

Somehow I knew I would have to ameliorate that position...blame it on the alcohol...a sudden half formed impulse but alright now. I could tell them the basic story, why not; it may work in my favour so long as I could skew it to 'drunk and upset' rather than 'disturbed and suicidal.' Would they want to contact Julia...and what about the note? I had not said anything clearly suicidal, though under the circumstances it would certainly be inferred.

My mind was in overdrive with all these things as we approached the hospital, and I was sobering up quickly. I knew that I would have to play the game, manage the situation, persuade them that it was a flash in the pan, all over, that they could feel OK about letting me go home.

A nurse introduced herself to me by her first name. She wasn't in uniform and talked to me in a casual, friendly manner, as if I might have been someone she'd been introduced to at a party. I was deposited in a carpeted waiting room with comfortable chairs which could have been anywhere, were it not for what was fairly obviously a sizeable two way mirror through to the nursing station. A coffee was on its way, as was the doctor. Fortunately the doctor was not as prompt as the coffee, which gave me more time to sober up and reflect.

It felt disarmingly easy-going here, but I cautioned myself again that I must not allow myself to *be* disarmed, which no doubt was the desired if not intentional effect. "Paranoid," I thought to myself…I was in the right place.

I was distracted from my despair, but wrapped it carefully, hid it away safely. It was mine and mine alone, my comfort, my secret. For now there were practicalities to attend to. A small but insistent voice was telling me to be patient, to wait, all would be well.

I was left in peace for the most part until the doctor arrived. He was accompanied by Michelle, the nurse who had welcomed me. He was a young Asian doctor who I estimated to be no more than twenty-five; doctors as well as policemen, I thought with a slight smile which he did not return, though I noticed him noticing; it had begun.

There were the usual details, background history, current circumstances and what they probably referred to as 'Precipitating factors,' and I followed the line I had decided on. I thought it went quite well, but the fact of my head having been on a railway line was a predictable fly in the proverbial ointment. Both the doctor and Michelle were disconcertingly direct in quizzing me about my suicidal intentions, planning and so forth, which strangely (considering the situation) I found a little surprising and somewhat rude, involving what would be considered in any other circumstance a degree of intrusiveness and indelicacy! Had I left a note? I said not.

This lack of obliqueness, the unsubtle approach, *was* disconcerting and made it harder to be evasive. Having to answer direct questions of this sort made greater demands on my ability to disguise my thoughts and feelings, and I was aware that they were observing me closely, my demeanour and how I said things as well as what I said. My initial confidence became shakier. I found myself at times sounding unconvincing, and at other times feeling that I just wanted to unburden myself, tell them the truth and have done with it. I was tired.

Somehow I held the line, and eventually they went away to confer. The bottom line had been that they wanted me to stay for a day or two at least to be properly assessed, and had canvassed whether I would be agreeable to do so. I was pretty reluctant to agree at first, but then divined as we went along that there were indeed (as I had suspected) powers to hold me anyway. These I gathered need not necessarily be invoked if they were reasonably confident that I would stay voluntarily...so of course I said yes...no problemo! Yes I could see that it did it seem sensible after all...silly me. A day or two I could hack. I'd easily convince them it was all a big mistake and I'd be on my way. I waited as if having been interviewed for a job, my prospective employers off to compare notes, weighing my merits and deficits.

They seemed a long time and I imagined the worst, but when they returned it was, as they say, a 'result.' I was to be allowed to remain voluntarily, and to be seen by the consultant psychiatrist the following day. I felt a little buzz off success. I recognized the feeling and realized that this was familiar territory, and that my twelve month apprenticeship in the art of deception might not be wasted here. I was equal to these people!

I was offered a bed in a room sharing with another patient who was fast asleep and snoring heavily. It was suffocatingly hot and impossible to sleep. The little success I had felt before faded rapidly as the reality of my situation closed in on me. I tossed and turned, cursing the snoring man, increasingly irked by my predicament...these people...do-gooders...what right had they!

I had to get away. I considered the fact that I was now a voluntary patient, and that there was actually nothing preventing me from changing my mind, from leaving. I would be polite but firm, cool and in control of myself, clearly no longer necessitating their concern. I would agree to call by tomorrow to see the consultant, but for now would call a taxi and take my leave. This was my first mistake.

At the nursing station which was, of course, by the exit door, I informed Michelle of my change of heart and good intentions for the morrow. There were two male nurses there also, and one accompanied Michelle and I into the waiting room to discuss my plan. It was very quickly evident that they were not going to allow me to leave, and they referred to 'nurses holding powers' which allowed them to detain me for up to two hours whilst a doctor was called to detain me for seventy-two. I quickly recanted apologized and agreed to stay; too late. The third nurse had bleeped the young Asian doctor who appeared much more promptly this time. I was detained under the mental health act, and given something to help me sleep.

Chapter 39

Dr Moor was a small compact woman 'of a certain age,' silver haired, posh Scottish, softly spoken. I could immediately appreciate how her empathic calmness of tone might be reassuring to an agitated disturbed person, but to me she posed a threat and I was on my guard. Perhaps this too was a mistake. My learning curve was growing ever steeper, and I was becoming more unsure of myself. I felt transparent, looked through as we discussed my misadventure. My explanations were solicitously appreciated, but we returned none the less and with a quiet inevitability to the railway line, my intentions, and my state of mind, which she drew from me with the gentle persistence of a leech.

Dr Moor was evidently a cautious woman, and not convinced by my attempts to reassure her. She wanted me to remain in hospital, and I tried to persuade her that it was not necessary, that I would happily take whatever medication she prescribed, that there would be no more incidents. I was trying too hard, talking too much, a contrived witticism or two…it wasn't working.

Her eyes were clear, grey, not unkindly but sharp, cutting through my defences so effortlessly. Never had I felt more exposed. I could see in her patient half smile that I was not succeeding, and found myself faltering, trying to remain calm and reasonable whilst hearing my own words clatter on stony ground. I had already tried to leave. My attempted suicide was serious, and she obviously suspected that I was spinning her a line, which of course I was. She'd been spun lines before.

By the time I saw that I would have to ameliorate my position, to agree to stay on voluntarily, it was already too late. I was not trusted, disbelieved. I needed to be assessed, understood, treated if necessary and made safe before I could be allowed to leave the hospital or indeed trusted to remain without compulsion. I was an IUD…an improvised unexploded device, and my wiring had to be examined. I had to be defused. Dr Moor was proposing to detain me for a further twenty eight days, and would arrange for a mental health social worker trained in the legal side to see me in order to approve the plan.

It was after lunch the following day when Basil Laird arrived. I'd made every effort in the meantime to appear 'normal,' chatting to the nurses and being pleasant and cooperative, if appropriately and genuinely somewhat down in the mouth, not to say depressed. When Basil Laird spent a little time in the nurses' station, presumably asking about me and checking the notes, I was slightly more optimistic, as I sensed that that they did not harbour the same level of concerns about me as Dr Moor did, and I felt that I might yet have a chance, if only I could persuade the social worker.

Basil Laird was a big man, a Scotsman, bluff and friendly. He asked me how it was going, commiserated and seemed genuinely sympathetic, which was nice. I joked with him that he must have come south to watch some decent football, and smiled at his riposte that he was actually doing some missionary work. I was encouraged.

I tried to appear relaxed and friendly, regretful and philosophical about what had happened, and thought I was doing alright. He was open about his purpose and didn't talk down to me, which encouraged me to think I could negotiate a deal here if I could only hold the line. I'd taken a bad knock …too much to drink…you know how it is…bloody stupid thing to do but alright now. He seemed a decent enough bloke and as we chatted I felt my confidence gaining traction, believed I could swing it.

He explained to me clearly his own professional responsibilities and my own rights, which he took pains to emphasise from the outset. I latched onto the phrase '…least restrictive option,' and pointed out my willingness to cooperate, to take the medicine, even to stay in hospital for a short while voluntarily. He listened attentively, sympathised, asked questions, reflected back to me the concerns felt by Dr Moor and (I was disappointed to hear) the nursing staff, and listened carefully to my replies. Ultimately he told me that he agreed that there was a real basis for the serious concerns, such that it would not be reasonable or safe to dispense with compulsory detention at this point. He informed me that I was detained under the mental health act on a twenty-eight day order.

Well it was a fair cop, but even in my reduced state as I was at the time, to be so comprehensively mistrusted and disbelieved was a considerable blow as it were to my professional pride, and I was going to have to play catch up. These people were not stupid. It caused be serious pause for thought in the days that followed, as I acclimatised to my new environment, determined to learn from what I perceived as my initial mistakes. I was going to have to be at the top of my game. I was down, but far from out, and learning fast.

Chapter 40

On Thursday two nurses accompanied me on a visit home to pick up some things. Much to my relief Julia had not returned early, and I was easily able to retrieve my note and shuffle it into the mail that I had picked up at the front door. It was strange being home. I felt nothing. It was already a past life from which I had severed any attachment, and I marvelled at this. I'd expected that going home would have affected me emotionally but it did not. I was calm, detached. I quickly gathered together a few things and we headed back.

No attachment. As we drove back to the hospital I considered the sudden unexpected freedom I felt. Suddenly there was clarity where there had been confusion. I was detained in a psychiatric hospital, but I was free, and I breathed and turned my attention inward as the car moved along. So different now to the journey in the police car, and words from my childhood came to me:

'Surely goodness and kindness shall follow me all the rest of my days.' Where did these words come from, echoing down the years? The flat, the hospital, neither was of any consequence. What did matter was the clarity of mind that contrasted so starkly with the driven and obsessive confusion that had seen me wreck my relationship with Julia, demean myself before Sian, and attempt to take my own life. I was lost, and now I was found.

Yes, I was different, changed. I had shed all attachments, was renewed and at one. It was the old cliché of the butterfly emerging from the chrysalis. A slowly dawning realization of my strength and well-being moved through me, spreading like a warming dram, and a small but assured voice consoled and encouraged...all would indeed be well!

I momentarily began to hum, but stopped as I noticed a look this attracted from one of the nurses. I needed to be careful. I had myself noticed fellow patients responding to hallucinations, often just distracted, looking rather than speaking, but easily recognisable to the nurses, even to me. I did not want them thinking this of me, or knowing anything about my state of mind. I had a part to play, one which would fulfil expectations and not raise suspicions in any way… depressed but getting better… getting over things…getting out!

How *should* I be now, returning from my estranged partner's home with a few things in a bag? I put my head in my hands, covering my eyes… a barely audible moan… a sigh:

"Oh god …"

"Are you OK?" One of the nurses put a solicitous hand on my arm.

"Yes…no…yes…oh I don't know, I suppose not. We were together a very long time. I just…don't know… "

"Sure. Look, just give it time… It'll take time. Just hang in…you'll see…it'll get better."

Yeah…I could *do* this! It wasn't like before, this was different, a quid pro quo, give these caring professional people what they wanted, what they needed , for me to have what I wanted, and we all would be happy.

The ward seemed such a casual, easy going place. It was different to how I would have expected it to be. There were no uniforms and there appeared to be very little in the way of structured, focussed 'therapy' going on, and only the most basic timetable for mealtimes, outside of which visitors wandered in and out much as they pleased. There were no groups other than some informal arts and crafts from time to time for anyone that was interested, and even one to one sessions with nurses generally resembled informal chats. Doctors would sometimes be around dealing with stuff that needed to be dealt with, but the doctors' main thing was the weekly ward round. There the consultant would hold court assisted by a junior, up-dated and guided by nursing staff. But the friendly nurses missed very little. They were the eyes and ears of the hospital, and the power behind the medical throne. Unwary patients (and sometimes *very* wary ones) were under constant surveillance in every situation, some unstable individuals on 'one to one'…a nurse within arm's length all the time or stationed with the door ajar outside their room. They observed, noted, discussed, hypothesised, and fed back to doctors who interviewed, diagnosed, treated, and made decisions about who should stay and who should go. I saw all this, and measured myself against them

The patients could be broadly split into two groups. There were the regulars, those poor souls who lived their illness all the time, needing refuge when things got particularly bad and the drugs needed to be fine-tuned. You could spot them a mile off, the old lags of the psychiatric system, though many not so old at all and still learning the ropes, more challenging, not yet burnt out and resigned to the half-light. The acute psychiatric ward was their normality, a home from home, which they would often rail against, but leave with trepidation… those that did. Then there were the new ones, those like me, brought here unexpectedly by some sudden and traumatic disintegration of their normality, strangers in a strange land, taking the medicine with always one eye on the door.

It was mostly quite calm, though there were outbursts and incidents too, but always quickly and professionally managed. It was far from the Victorian 'Bedlam,' and bore little resemblance to Nurse Ratchet's highly controlled totalitarian regime. It was benign and reasonable, but a place of careful study designed to uncover the hidden processes of disturbed human minds. It was a place where it would be difficult to hide.

I took to walking in the hospital grounds where there were lawns and well-tended borders and shrubberies. Spring was in full bloom, and it was pleasant to sit on one of the many benches dotted about. At first I had to have a nurse with me, but after just a few days was allowed to go by myself. I sometimes took a notepad, having taken to writing down my thoughts about what I had gone through. It seems a little strange describing it like that: 'what I had gone through,' but it did now seem to me that it had been an ordeal. Writing it down, re-visiting it in this way was a strange journey, and filled some of the endless hours on the ward when I would retreat to my room and scribble away.

I could remember it all very well, the thoughts, the feelings, but there on the page in front of me it seemed like someone else's story, and not someone I would associate with myself, or would like to. There was the bit from that psalm that we always had in school, 'If I should walk in the valley of darkness no evil should I fear.' Not that I'd 'got god' or anything like that, or really thought of it as evil, but the sense of the valley of darkness was tangible, and when I thought of how my life had been derailed, how I had been taken over by sex... lust, I could not help but also bring to mind the bit from the Lord's Prayer, '...and lead us not into temptation.' I knew exactly what this was.

I had rapidly arrived at two decisions. The first was that I would outwardly cooperate completely. I demurred on Basil Laird's suggestion that I could, even *should*, appeal against my detention. I recanted on any resistance to being in hospital, placing myself entirely in the hands of the doctors and nurses, bowing to their wisdom and expertise. The second decision was quite simply that they should know nothing of my true thoughts. I would be a master of disguise. There would be no more mistakes.

Chapter 41

"You daft cunt." It was midway through the second week, and I had a visitor…Ray.

"Yeah, that's why I'm here!"

He handed me a bag of grapes with a flourish.

"There ye go."

"Oh, grapes; ta; that's original."

"Yeah, well, I'm a traditionalist really, beneath my off beat avant-garde persona."

We were sitting in the reception room, and Ray had already clocked the mirror.

"Yeah," I said, "Let's go out on the terrace…it's a bit more private."

It was a sunny morning and there were one or two other patients outside smoking. Everybody here smoked. We walked along to the far end where we could be by ourselves on a bench under the pink canopy of a large cherry tree.

"How did you find out I was here?"

"Well with some difficulty being as your phone's switched off. I was leaving you to stew but Julia rang my mobile at the weekend… said you were AWOL and I got a bit windy…with good cause it would seem."

"Oh, so you know about…"

"About the railway line…yeah…that was doing it in style my boy."

I felt slightly embarrassed, but grateful too for his care, for being able to have a normal conversation with a good friend, one that I certainly didn't deserve.

"Yeah, well I always did like trains. Used to be a train spotter when I was a kid."

He laughed. "I can imagine. What were you doing, trying to get the tyre size as it went past?"

We ate some grapes. The silence between us was easy.

"How *is* Julia?" I said. "Did she say about…"

"Oh she said alright. Thought you may have eloped with Sian…I had to pretend not to know…bloody awkward for me. "

 I fidgeted, now that the subject had come up. "Yeah. Sorry about that."

"Mmmmmmm." He helped himself to some grapes.

"Anyway, Julia's not best pleased…I hope you're not expecting to…"

 "Oh no, don't worry Ray, I know the score."

We both gazed up into the confetti branches. "Here!" I said," how come Julia had your mobile?"

Ray looked suddenly serious. "Look I don't quite know how to say this, so I'm just going to lay it on the line. Me and Julia've been having weekly assignations down the Midland Hotel since Christmas."

 My mouth dropped open. "You haven't?!"

"Fucking hell Callum leave it out will you! You really are barmy aren't you?"

My turn to laugh. "Go on then, so how did you track me down to here?"

 "Oh, not too difficult really, just rang the boys in blue."

"What and they told you I had my head on a railway line…on the bloody blower…so much for confidentiality. I'm going to put in a complaint!"

"So what's the score here then?" Ray was serious now, business like, cutting to the chase.

"I'm stuck here for twenty-eight days while they get my number...well, less if I'm good. *Detained* they call it. Sounds quite pleasant really doesn't it? "Pardon me sir; may I just detain you for a month or so?" Stuck me on antidepressants. It's going OK though. They seemed pretty positive when the doc saw me yesterday. It won't go beyond the twenty-eight."

This was true. The feedback *had* been positive, and I knew from what Basil Laird had said that they would need to be able to make a good case to a tribunal to detain me any longer, which I now felt I would be easily able to oppose by the time a month had passed.

Ray was looking at me studiously now.

"You're different Callum. What is it? I thought you'd be in bits."

What was it Sian had said...sharp?

"Yeah, well, I was at first...but they rebuilt me...stronger...faster..."

"Yeah?" He chimed in. "Lean and hungry eh?"

"Well...not so hungry any more Ray."

"No," he said. "Not surprising really. Fingers slightly burned." He said it in a matter of fact way. There really was no animosity, which I wondered at and appreciated, suddenly wanting to trust him; there had to be someone.

"No it's not that Ray. It's, well, it's that I've come through all that...I've found goodness."

Immediately his look changed. I saw Dr Moor's studied gaze and quickly changed tack.

"Give me a break you daft bastard, course they're burned, and not just my fingers...oh, sorry...I didn't mean..."

His face relaxed. "Yeah I know. Ye didn't but ye did. I *was* slightly pissed off about it, but it was quite amusing too in a sadistic sort of way, so don't feel too bad."

He helped himself to some grapes and chewed them leaning back and looking up into the tree. I took some too.

"Mmmmmmm...nice these."

"Yeah. I mean it's not as if I didn't know, and to be honest I had a ringside seat...well more the Coliseum than Billy Smarts...and you were *not* the lion old son. I did try to warn you Callum."

I sighed, remembering very well. "Yeah. I know."

"Course, I didn't know about Julia then."

We both ate some grapes. At last it had been aired and dealt with in our own blokish way. We weren't going to talk about the baby. We weren't going to talk about my suicide attempt. There was no need.

"So what now then...Julia wants you to get a solicitor and sort out the chattels. Any idea where you're going to live?"

We discussed practicalities. I told him to let Julia know that she could have the flat, just to get the paperwork drawn up and I'd sign it. I waved aside his objections. I'd thought about it and it was a decision already made. Restitution of a kind perhaps, but the greater part of the flat was hers anyway, and I would never be able to make up for her loss. Ray said he had one or two useful contacts in the property line and he'd find me a small furnished place for now. The hospital would help me get my benefits sorted out.

Quiet now. Pink petals fluttering to the ground in ones and twos, or in little showers where a bird disturbed the blossom.

"You don't love her do you Ray?"

It was almost as if he'd expected the question...at least he didn't show the slightest surprise. He humphed, smiled, looked down at his knees and carefully brushed away a petal that had settled on his jeans.

"I understand her Callum," he said, looking straight ahead. He wasn't finished and I waited as he weighed his words. "We're two of a kind. We know one another. That's the way it is." I sensed a punch line and it came, thrown away at last, Ray turning to me with a knowing smile: "...and she's a great fuck."

Chapter 42

Ray's visit affected me, both the fact that he had visited at all, and the things that it caused to rise to the surface. I hadn't expected to see him, and despite him having known about it all, I still felt that I had done him a great wrong, and was touched by his loyalty and forgiveness.

It felt around that time as if I was looking through a window into my former life as if it was somebody else's. I was able to appreciate the happiness that was there as well as the mistakes that I'd made, without actually feeling the joy or the pain. I thought of Julia with affection, no, with love, but without regret. She was a good woman who had not deserved to be treated as I had treated her or to have suffered such loss as a result; but I had no regret. I believed that her life would be better without me. I was glad of the opportunity to give her my part of the flat, and would ensure that she knew that other matters were attended to also, which would relieve her pain.

I thought of Sian and smiled as I remembered her performances and our sexual cavorting. It was an indulgent smile, a smile that an adult might make to a child who had eaten too much ice cream and made himself sick. I did not recognise the person that was me who had played the male role in this real life passion play, and could not begin to connect with the overwhelming feelings which had held such power over me. I laughed as I felt the familiar arousal thinking of her still evoked; I was still a man after all, and it amused me that I had risen above though not entirely beyond my own base humanity...and was rising still! I looked around quickly to ensure that my laugh had not been noticed.

No, there were no regrets, and neither did I feel any bitterness toward anyone. It was over, all of it, a different me, a different time. I felt sorry for people, Jules, Ray, Sian, the patients, the staff, endlessly caught up in the struggle from which I had moved free.

As well as my walks in the hospital grounds, I was already having accompanied trips into town for coffee. I'd been given to understand that I would soon be able to go to town alone, and felt at one with myself, patient, and looking forward to my discharge.

Dr Moor still had me taking the antidepressants, and I'd agreed to carry on with them. Well she seemed to be pleased that I was taking her pills, as doctors tend to be, but it was really a safety net. My mood had improved so well that she concluded my depression was of the reactive type and had not descended into the dark depths of a major clinical disorder. The 'incident' was an alcohol fuelled aberration…an impulsive and extreme response to a life crisis. Doubtless she also thought, I surmised, that if this were the case she must think me a rather shallow individual. I didn't mind, but I knew different, that I was a man of truly hidden depths.

But no, Dr Moor was no fool, and I could see that she had her doubts. She knew she would struggle to hold onto me, but wasn't in any hurry to let me go either. She regularly would ask me leading questions about my thoughts, gently probing, looking for clues with that look that said: "You're too good to be true." I felt strangely close to her, my dancing partner in a deadly game, and she could see it in my eyes.

Chapter 43

Altogether I was in hospital for a month, though it felt much longer. I don't mean that it was tedious, though it surely could be tedious at times; I mean it much more positively than that. It was a period of reflection, communion, consolidation, growth.

Outwardly I played the game, but not with the impelled troubled urgency that I used to in the days of my affair. It was a careful, controlled performance, the professional gambler now, as opposed to the talented amateur tilting at the odds.

Nobody was hurt in this particular game, and I was glad about that. Indeed I perceived a good deal of obliqueness, deftness of touch, even subtly encouraged entrapment by my medical friends, which approximated to sleight of hand in any case, and I viewed them as worthy opponents and fair game.

Ray was a good friend to me, visiting me regularly and taking me out as time went on. One of these trips was to view a small flat he'd found for me. Flatlet would probably have been a better way to describe it, more than a bedsit but with an open plan layout more to do with making the best use of a lack of space than with modern design. Still, it was nicely furnished and cheap, and Ray pointed out that it should be thought of as a starter pack whilst I found my feet.

I gratefully took it, and was allowed to visit and buy a few things. Julia had been very prompt with the paperwork for me to sign for the flat, and Dr Moor had written a letter to confirm that I had the capacity to make the decision, though she didn't think I was being very sensible and tried to persuade me to wait. Well, perhaps she wouldn't think me so shallow after all. The upshot was that Julia was forthcoming with various bits and pieces for my new home which Ray ferried over for me. I told him there was no need but he was suddenly clucking around like a mother hen so I let him get on with it.

Sian visited too, just one time, out of the blue one murky Manchester afternoon. I was reading in my room when Chris, one of the nurses, popped his head round the door: "Visitor for you Callum...Sian Davies...? She's in reception if you want to see her." I looked blank, thrown by the surname and taking a second to register. "You do know Sian...?"

"Oh... Sian! Sorry Chris. Yes. I was just...I'll be right along." He gave me a very unprofessional wink and disappeared.

I walked along to the reception room and immediately saw the reason for the wink. Poised on expensive pastel pink stilettos Sian had dressed, how can I put it, with a great deal of thought. She looked stunningly sexy, a tight cream silk skirt with an obligingly generous split up the side, and an ivory sweater, ultra-fine cashmere that clung like a second skin to her bra-less breasts. Some tasteful simple jewellery, Gautier watch...the high class hooker look, chic but openly provocative. I had to smile, though in that first moment I also felt sad for her, even with my cock springing obediently to life as she kissed me softly on the cheek.

"Hello Callum." I had forgotten what her voice sounded like, and there was the familiar perfume too.

"Hello Sian", I said, still smiling broadly and hoping that I didn't appear to be mocking, or worse still mad! "This is a nice surprise." It was rather limp, I thought...the only thing that was.

"Yes," she said, still standing facing me, seemingly neither of us quite knowing what to do next.

"Grab a seat," I said motioning to her to sit. My chair was almost at right angles to Sian's, and immediately I was treated to an impressive expanse of thigh above her lace stocking tops as she crossed her legs, affecting with deliberate lack of conviction to be innocently unaware of her wilful and mischievous temptation; this had the inevitable effect of course of making it all the more tempting. Sian was an artiste.

"Callum..." she hesitated and her composure faltered. "Callum I'm a bitch. I'm really sorry."

I could see that she really meant it, as far as she ever really meant anything. There was a soft liquid glint in her eye, and I understood that this was really it... why she had come...to say sorry. But the other agenda was irrepressible. She could not leave it to one side, function without sexuality.

I knew that the 'accidental' display was deliberate, and she knew that I did. I sensed her arousal...well it was obvious when I looked at her tits...and I *was* looking... I HAD to look. This was the point. Does that make me a hypocrite? Well maybe; but for Sian this was both her power and her chain. I saw this clearly now, and though my cock was hard fit to burst, felt only sorrow for this woman who I had thought I loved, but who could not do this one well-meant thing without all the rest.

"It's OK Sian, honestly. It was me as much as you. We both had our demons; and listen, I really do appreciate you coming here today, saying what you said. You know I think you are a good person."

I felt her power, and my own awkwardness like some kind of born again happy clappy who didn't yet know the script properly and was not fully convinced or convincing. And yet I was sincere. I was aware how clumsy what I said might have sounded, pompous even, but it wasn't meant to be like that. I wasn't trying to save a fallen woman or to be better than her. I was trying to appeal to the better side of her, the part she kept hid, perhaps because she didn't really know what to do with it.

I was talking to the Sian who had come to say sorry, to make amends, hoping that maybe with just a few words, a shift of focus, I could help her; but she could see my hard on, looked long and longingly at it and smiled, eyebrow raised as her eyes met mine again, failing to hear me, except for the opportunity to extract a little innuendo. "Well you always said I was."

"What?"

"You always said I was: 'good,' Callum."

"Yes," I said, quietly. I just did not know what to say, and realized I was smiling again, bemused, exasperated, wanting her to be different too...to understand; but to Sian I was a man with an erection, a man who wanted her, who she had made to want her, and I had looked at her just as she wanted me to... despite myself.

We sat in silence and my eyes drifted to the carpet. I could sense her composure, waiting, confident in her irresistible charms. They had never let her down before...or perhaps they always had.

"Callum." She intoned softly, leaning slightly toward me, gratified to have my eyes on her once more, not noticing that I was far away. She casually swept her gaze across the mirror, tossed her hair back in the way I knew so well, and her eyes fixed on mine. "I don't suppose you have your own room, do you?"

That was the last time I saw Sian.

Chapter 44

At last I was home. It was all a bit of an anti-climax really. There was no send off, just a quick goodbye to the nurses and one or two of the patients who happened to be around, and I headed off with my bag and caught the bus.

He didn't say anything to me until we got home, Baby, but I knew of course that he was with me. I made a cup of filter coffee, put the pot on the little coffee table and sat quietly. I waited for his little voice, here with me in my flat, away from prying eyes and ears. Now I could acknowledge him freely, now after all this time we were alone together.

"I told you it would all be alright Daddy," he said at last.

"Yes," I said, "You did and you were right…I knew, too." I sipped my coffee contentedly, feeling him close. No need for any more pretence, deception, lies.

"And Daddy," he said, pausing then, waiting for me to respond, enjoying our new freedom as much as I was.

"What is it Baby?"

"I love you," he replied.

"I know you do, and I love you Baby." There was a silence then, suffused with the warmth of our love.

"Daddy," he said at last.

 I sipped my coffee. "Mmmm?"

"When are you going to come and look after me?"

"I drained the cup and put it down. "Soon Baby, very soon. I just have to write to Mummy…to tell her we love her…to tell her we're alright."

Chapter 45: Epilogue

This was Callums story. It was Ray who found him. He'd gone round that night with a bottle to celebrate. When he got no reply and the mobile was off he'd sensed the worst. Ray *was* sharp, but this time it was too late. He kicked the door in and found Callum hanging in the living room. There was a letter on the table for me.

He'd bought a drill and a heavy bracket, screwed it to a ceiling joist, nothing left to chance; probably the first bit of DIY he'd ever done; it was a good job.

I talked a lot to Ray, at the time and since. He took it hard. Sian lit out when she heard the news, some Greek island for a fortnight, I later heard… didn't attend the funeral and nothing sent. She'd kept a diary and hadn't stinted on the detail…all the emotional games too…stuff she hadn't told Ray. She must have forgotten it in her rush. Ray found it when she was away; he packed up her things and put them into storage. That was that. I never saw her again.

Ray didn't want to give me the diary, said he'd wished he hadn't mentioned it, but I prised it from him, eventually, when I was just about over things. I had Callums notepads anyway, I told him, and he hadn't left much out. Callums account was different though…shades of a 'misspent youth,' coming to terms… an apology of sorts, and despite it all I felt his love. The diary knocked me back, I have to say, hearing it in her voice, the woman who took him from me. I began writing things down, trying to piece it all together, to make sense of it all.

So, here it is. How many women would have put themselves up for all this…the intimate details and, let's face it, second fiddle by a long chalk!? Perhaps it's my catharsis; working it through, *being* him, filling in the gaps; filling in the void in my life, that vacuum in my centre where the baby briefly was, where Callum had been for all those years, when we'd sparred and made love, talked about a holiday in Cordoba.

Perhaps it is at some level an atonement, acknowledging it all, not just that, putting it out there. Not that I feel responsible, guilty, not that. No, I'm not taking on *that* burden. It was after all Callum who had been playing around, lying through his back teeth. Call it what you like...a cautionary tale, an epitaph to the man I loved and who loved me, and who I failed. Because he was a child; I always knew that, and looked after him, kept him right. But in the end, to use one of his own favourite phrases, I '...took my eye off the ball.'

Ray's still around, still on his own, like me, and we're still friends, good friends. We're over things now and we don't often speak about it, but there will always be that connection, that sense of needless loss, of something either one of us could have done, maybe should have.

This year I went to Cordoba in May, for my birthday. It was much as I'd imagined. The narrow streets in the old city, the Mezquita, its flaky sandstone ramparts baking in the Andalucian sun, and a thousand Moorish arches perched on pillaged pillars in its cool inner cloisters. And of course, there was the patio festival, the little hidden gardens, bursting with spring flowers and the music of fountains. It *was* good.

One morning I'd given up on sleep, and taking a stroll around the quiet streets before breakfast had wandered into a lovely little courtyard with a dazzling array of flowers in pots and hanging baskets. It was still quite early and the soft spring sunshine played on the recently hosed dripping plants, and slanted shadows ran across the patio, the puddles and pretty mosaics, gathering beneath the enclosing colonnade. A freshness pervaded the morning air, and I could hear sounds of the family somewhere breakfasting. Even here there were beautiful arches set on polished marble pillars, and a pretty little fountain, its one simple jet lazily tumbling back upon itself. I was alone.

A young chattering couple entered, French, and to my mind annoyingly so, intruding on my moment and breaking the spell. He was very tall and slim and moved with a slow lugubrious grace like a heron, whist she was the opposite…petite, compact, her movements quick and precise, an odd pairing yet somehow they fitted together well. Before I could make my escape they asked me if I would take their photo by the fountain, smiling and trying their English, so that I immediately regretted my petty peevishness and agreed.

As they stood by the fountain the young man struck a pose, prompting a scolding from his partner and a rapid fire interchange followed as she remonstrated with him and he feigned innocence. The French was too fast for me, but I got the gist, as the ball was comically batted back and forth between them. I was momentarily forgotten, but then they suddenly recalled themselves and both turned to me to seek my allegiance and support with palms presented in simultaneous Gallic shrugs which I caught perfectly with a well-timed click of the shutter.

They loved the picture and laughed, she raising her hand to her mouth with a little exclamation, and he clearly taking the opportunity to get his own back regarding *her* silly pose.

I offered to take another: "It's very funny, but would you like me to take one that *isn't* silly?"

But the young man wouldn't hear of it: "Mais non…no…it is perfect…silly yes, but then we *are* silly, so perhaps it is the camera that is telling the truth!"

The girl's mouth dropped theatrically agape and she accosted him once more. She gesticulated indicating the two of them: "What? *We* are silly…vraiment? Tu m'accuse? C'est toi qui est l'enfant ici! Je ne pense pas que c'est moi…." and the machine gun French rattled on until he slipped his arm around her shoulders and now playfully but firmly pressed his free hand against her mouth as she squealed, struggling to free herself.

"Please…excuse my wife…she is… how do you say it…not quite herself today?"

They were holding hands and kissing as they took their leave, and I felt the familiar tug on my never quite healed heart as I trailed my fingers in the cool water and watched them depart.

Yes, it *was* good; but I could not help wondering how it might have been.

Printed in Great Britain
by Amazon